IN SEARC

In Search of Mihailo

DOLORES PALÀ

Allison & Busby
Published by W. H. Allen & Co. Plc

An Allison & Busby book
Published in 1989 by
W.H. Allen & Co. Plc
Sekforde House
175/9 St John St
London EC1V 4LL

First published in Great Britain by Allison & Busby in 1969

Printed in Great Britain by
Courier International Ltd, Tiptree, Essex

ISBN 0 85031 860 2

For Christy

Chapter One

THE church is large and impersonal, 1930 gothic. Through my own numbness in getting out of the taxi and slowly walking up the steps to the entrance, through my own walled numbness I felt a certain curiosity for the aunt whose funeral this was. A certain curiosity for the familiar stranger who had died and left me a considerable amount of money. And who had become a Roman Catholic somewhere along the line. But the touch or flash of curiosity was no more than that, a flicker breaking through a wall around myself, a tight high wall of fear, a grotesque wall around myself. Keeping out the image of Paris, keeping out the noise and smell, the sight of Paris, keeping out the reality that I am here, that this is where we will now get to the end of the road, that this is where we will find out, and in finding out we will come to the end.

The lawyer greeted me at the door of the church. He looked at me sharply, taking my pallor for grief yet not quite convinced of grief in proportion to such pallor. Sharp little Auvergnat, Maître Jeanson. Yesterday he telephoned me in London and told me in his correct English that my aunt Alice had died. In her sleep. Peacefully.

"My dear Mrs. Davies, your aunt thought so highly of you. She left you a considerable sum of money. In the order of twenty-five thousand dollars."

He waited for my reaction, my gasp of surprise; the timing of a professional speech-maker. Funny little Aunt Alice. Imagine her having twenty-five thousand dollars to leave.

"You will want to attend the funeral, of course," he continued. "I shall do my best to arrange all the preliminary paper-work for the same day. You can sign a power of attorney . . ."

And his voice droned on at six shillings a minute, but I was no longer listening.

As though from a distance I heard my own voice answering: "No, no. I will not go to Paris. You know I never go to Paris. No, I cannot. . . . Out of the question. . . . I am very sorry . . . no . . . no . . . it cannot be done. . . . I simply never go to Paris . . ."

Thank God Gavin was not there. He would have been furious with me, with the resurgence of what he called my "Paris mania", furious and impatient at my rejection of logic in this matter.

"No . . . I cannot come. Surely I can sign it here. . . . Please . . . there must be a way. . . . I know. . . . Yes. . . . I know. . . . A great deal of money. . . . Yes . . . very kind indeed. . . . Yes. . . ."

Slowly, his argument stronger than mine, which was no argument, slowly at six shillings a minute long distance, the exasperated Maître Jeanson had my promise that I would arrive on the nine a.m. plane at Le Bourget and would come immediately to St. Joseph's Church on the Avenue Hoche, the English-speaking Catholic Church. I would be free no later than the following day. He guaranteed it. What hotel would I like? Hotel? And my heart began to pound. Why must I go through this now? Why do I have to be dragged back now, after all these years? What hotel? I don't know. The Cayré? Fine. Fine. One night, no more.

I sat staring at the telephone for some time afterwards. Knowing that I would be in Paris again; knowing that the time had come to find out; to close the parentheses.

I live in a pretty Georgian house in Chelsea. My husband is Gavin Davies. He is an architect. We have four sons. Gavin and I have been married since 1953. We met in New York and lived there for a few years. In 1955 we moved back to England. I lead an active, healthy life, surrounded by active, healthy people. I love my children, my husband, my home; I have friends and enough money not to have to worry about it. Life is full and pleasant and I am aware of it, sometimes painfully so.

Yet this life that I began in 1953 with Gavin is the result of another life, an incomplete one, which I had left three years earlier. I left it or it left me?

Here within St. Joseph's Church, the narrow gothic of 1930 blinking at me, Maître Jeanson's hand on my arm, on the slow walk down to the front pews, other pews scattered with elderly American ladies and their faded husbands, looking at me curiously, Aunt Alice's only family in Europe. So pale, one said, so pale.

The harsh organ crashed out, startling me with its size. Priests appeared at the altar. Aunt Alice's coffin is covered with a great blanket with a T for Thorpe. There is a smell of incense and the high requiem mass booms out deafeningly around me. My knuckles are white. The choir sings quite beautifully.

Years ago in a small Connecticut church Tor was prayed for, but there was no priest, no incense, no Swiss Guards with scepters and ribbons, no Mozart Requiem, no voices raised but my own silent voice, nothing but the whimper of my own silence; left behind.

Thirteen years ago Tor, my father, was only forty-four. I had been in Paris two years when Tor called me home. I didn't want to leave, to go to him. Not till I realised he was dying. And how slowly the realisation came. Tor could not die! Not at forty-four. Golden-haired Tor, young and laughing Tor, the most amusing, the most alive of men. Dying of a cancer that might have been cured a year before.

Indestructible Tor ravaged by pain and death. I went home and sat with him through months of fear and anguish, through months of morphine and agony. Until finally he died and everything died with him.

And this is Paris again. Back to the beginning, back to the first days, back to the source. In the cool scented church the priest spreads his arms before the tabernacle while the mourners kneel and I mourn that other death of long ago.

Last night in London I went about the business of leaving my children for two days. I called a friend who agreed to come over and stay in the house. I got the maid to wait until after dinner to leave, later than usual. My husband, ironically enough, is in Ireland and will not return until tomorrow or the next day. I left the lawyer's telephone number and the name of the hotel where I would be staying. I packed a bag with a change of clothes and a Spanish shawl to wear at the funeral. I went to bed early, taking two Seconals, and slept until seven in the morning. It seemed to me, looking at myself from outside, that I was very calm. Yet it was a curious calm, an almost frightening calm. In the morning light my steps on the glossy airport floors sounded cold and inhuman to my ears. The glimpse I caught of myself in a mirror showed a tall woman in a black suit with a very pale face, a woman who looked as though she were starting off on a long journey, not an hour's ride across the Channel. I looked at the reflection with interest; for a second I found it hard to believe it was me.

But the deceptive, the spurious calm evaporated at Le Bourget. On the way into the city the taxi driver took the rue de Flandre, and I felt my stomach grow tight with fear within me. I kept my eyes closed, or focused on the seat, or on the handle of my black-and-white travelling bag, far from the rue de Flandre which I knew so well. I closed myself off from Paris, from people's faces, from the way they walked on the streets, from the sounds of their voices or the screechings of their cars.

Once in the church, the music soaring above me, under the gentle eyes of the elderly ladies, a comfort, Maître Jeanson's watchful presence at my side, I felt safe again. My tears confused the outlines of the priests. The coffin floundered before my eyes. Not for Aunt Alice, not for that kind old lady, but for my own coffin, my own coffinless funeral so long ago when I buried myself after my father in Connecticut and began a new life which had nothing to do with the one I had known before. I was born at the age of twenty-two.

The mass is over. We walk behind the coffin, Maître Jeanson and I, to the rear of the church. The elderly ladies and their husbands shake hands with me. The ritual is strange and unfamiliar. I recognise no one, shaking hands automatically, accepting condolence for another death.

In the car going to the cemetery Maître Jeanson asked me how long it had been since I had visited Paris. "Thirteen years," I replied. I never came back. Never again. Yet I am here now and now it will end. Now I will know everything. I will make myself find out. I will make myself be strong enough to find out. I will look for him and for . . . myself? No. Not for myself. I will find myself in him. In the way he was, in what he has become. I will know. I must know.

Suddenly, all the silence of all these years, all the countless times I did not cry out Mihailo, where are you, what in Christ's name happened? all the hundreds of times I never mentioned his name, all those first hideous years when I picked my way through life, carefully keeping my mind in a straight line, like a tight-rope walker in a high wind, all through those first years of panic and despair and cold—even in New York's hottest summers I was cold, because inside

5

I was dead, keeping that balance was my sole concern, all those years fell away at my feet. Now. I will find out now.

Though there has been no panic for a long time, there has been something dead inside me, something atrophied, a part of me that ceased to function as a result of Tor's death, of Mihailo's vanishing. For that was what it was: vanishing. The shock both these losses wrought on me caused a curious state of mind bordering on madness at first, eventually settling into a dull, empty, detached resignation. Until Gavin. Healthy Gavin, who said one afternoon in Central Park, "My dear girl, what you need is a houseful of children and I propose to start one right now!" Gavin, the antithesis of self-indulgence, the eternal giver, the gentlest of men, the most impatient critic of what he called "Greenwich Village cerebral masturbation", the wisest of husbands. He all but shook me back to earth. Thank God. Yet even Gavin never fought my refusal to return to Paris. One is never all that sure.

But now I am here and I will know. Standing at the grave near the lawyer and the priest, I moved a little to one side and said aloud, to myself, as though I were praying, "Mihailo, I have come back to find you." Just to hear my own voice.

We walked down the cemetery rows, newly green in the mild May sunlight.

Maître Jeanson said to me with a theatrical sigh, "You see, it was not too painful, was it? Now we shall go to my office where I will will begin to explain matters to you. Then we can have a bit of lunch somewhere. In the afternoon most of the papers will be ready to go to the Embassy and tomorrow morning you will have the power of attorney. By late afternoon you should be able to sign and leave. Perhaps earlier. It will all be quite easy, I assure you."

I listened to him carelessly, noting only that I would be free by early afternoon. Wells of panic surged up in me again. It is not all that simple. You do not just drop the coats of mail you have carefully built around a part of you, you do not just drop them like that, because of one of those curious accidents of fate, such as Aunt Alice's death in Paris. Not after thirteen years! It came with such force again, the surge of panic, that I missed a step. The lawyer's hand reached out to steady me. Yet I kept feeling fear rush through me like electric currents. This is the end of the affair. I felt drained of strength, drained of all resources. I cannot go through with it. I will not be able to.

During the rest of the morning, during an endless lunch somewhere near the Champs Elysées, looking at Paris from taxis or from Jeanson's office windows, or at the notary section of the American Embassy at the Place de la Concorde, I felt dizziness overcome me a hundred times. I felt the impossible presence of my own ghost in this noisy city and all over again I saw Mihailo's tall silhouette in his shabby raincoat with the frayed sleeves, his incredibly luminous smile. I saw him in a hundred corners of the streets, at each turn of the taxi, at every door about to be opened, till finally at the end of the proceedings I felt the exhaustion of the near-insane and wanted only to go to whatever hotel Jeanson had chosen for me, to go there and to go to bed and to cry into an anonymous pillow, alone. Dizzily, then, the long afternoon drew itself out, and mechanically I let myself be put into still another taxi and the hotel was finally reached.

I lay down on the bed and slept almost immediately. An hour or so later I woke up, much calmer. The fact that the hotel was on Boulevard Raspail had escaped my attention; I only noticed it then, written on an ashtray. So. Montparnasse again. I ran a hot bath and relaxed in the water, smoking a cigarette. This must stop. I must come to terms with myself. There must be an end to all this. But all I could see was the beginning, fifteen years earlier.

Chapter Two

I WAS home for Christmas holidays in 1947, home with Tor in his house in Connecticut, where he taught in a small college. I was nineteen and an art student. I had been looking at a book of poetry Tor published during the war. There was a poem dedicated to Paris, then occupied.

"When can I go to Paris, Tor?" I asked. He looked up startled.

"Do you want to go?"

"Several kids from the League left in September. They are at the Grande Chaumière and with Leger or Lhote. They're doing much more than we are here."

"You're a bit young, don't you think?" he answered, looking at me musingly.

We did not talk about it any more that day but the next evening at dinner Tor brought it up again.

"About Paris. I've been thinking. Finish out this year at the League. If you still want to go you could sail in June. Monique and Fred Brooks could look after you, I guess. You'll be almost twenty, then. I suppose that's no longer as young as it used to be." He grinned. "I'll arrange everything."

That was just what he did, arrange everything. He used to spend summers in Europe before the war, while I spent them with my mother. She and Tor were divorced when I was five. Tor brought me up; my childhood was happiness itself, the image of Tor.

As the month of June 1948 drew nearer, Tor's plans for me became more concrete. I had been accepted at the Grande Chaumière, Monique and Fred Brooks and Monique's son

Claude Gallien were expecting me. I had letters of introduction to everyone Tor had ever known in Paris who might be of help to a twenty-year-old art student—introductions which turned out to be to half of Saint-Germain-des-Prés.

I sailed on the *de Grasse* on June 5th, and was met at the Gare Saint-Lazare in Paris by a tall, gangling young man in a blazer and grey flannels, looking very English and bearing a cardboard sign reading "Miss Thorpe Please." The sign was glued onto the kind of stick that goes with children's balloons.

I looked at him, burst out laughing, and said, "Claude Gallien?"

He examined me for a minute and answered in an Evelyn Waugh voice, "Well, that's not too bad. I was afraid you'd turn out to be that lady philologist over there with the moustache and boots. Come along, we'll try to get you out of customs now." He flicked the sign onto a passing luggage carrier, to the noisy indignation of the porter.

Claude, who is so close to me today and who was there at the beginning. I can still see that first day in Paris. I can still feel the disbelief that it all wasn't a dream, the amazing wonderland that was Paris in 1948.

Remember Paris in 1948. Remember the streets, the cafés, the *caves*, the songs, the *boîtes*, the bars, the food, the smell, the air. Remember that tall young Claude, so English, so lanky, laughing in his dandyfied way, his stinging wit, his enormous kindness, his exuberance, his joy. Remember me with him in those first few months.

With Claude I walked up the streets of Paris in 1948, underheated, underfed, exhilarating Paris, beautiful under the grime of the war years, come out from under, alive and healthy, old yet renewed. In 1948.

We drove across to the room he had rented for me on the rue du Dragon. It was in the apartment of a deaf old widow, Madame Ferson. The room was big and bright, overlooking the street. High up on the fourth floor I saw for the first time the crazy-quilt beauty of Paris roofs. The room was perfect. I was entitled to use the kitchen and a bath cost eighty francs extra. My rent was roughly about fifteen dollars a month.

With Claude and me it was a kind of love at first sight, but not a physical one. From the very first I think we knew; surveying each other in the sun-filled room on the rue du Dragon, amid the trunks and suitcases, the bright red cabbage roses of the bedspread, we instinctively recognised that we had found a remarkable friendship.

"There are two quarters," he explained, perched on a chair watching me try to unpack. "That is, two that you will find count more than the others. Montparnasse and Saint-Germain-des-Prés. The Latin Quarter, which Americans tend to confuse with everything else, is more student-ish, but it is not to be dismissed. Ghosts of François Villon and Rutebeuf and all that. But Saint-Germain, where you live and Montparnasse, where your school is, are the centre of things. Then there is the Right Bank. After which we can also visit Brussels and Leeds if you like. . . . "

I sat down on a pile of clothes, laughing with him. "Don't you ever cross the river? Is it like New Yorkers who have never been further west than the Museum of Modern Art?"

"No," he grinned, "I'm exaggerating. But you get the point."

"Tell me about you. You're French but you were brought up in England, Tor told me. He also said your father was killed in the war."

"My father taught at the Lycée Français in London. We

moved to London when I was three. You'll be interested to know that I've got a bloody awful English accent in French. Yes, my father was killed in forty-two. My mother, whom you'll love, is now married to Fred Brooks, the English painter. They live in the Midi, in the hills above Cannes. Fred, God bless him, is one of those English rarities—he still has some money left. Do you know his work?"

"No. Should I?"

"Well, the mother country and all that. Do you only see American painters in the States?"

I laughed. He made America seem tiny and exotic, like New Zealand.

"Anyway, you'll know it soon enough. He's not half bad. And a very good chap. Spanish war and that sort of thing. Big, vague fellow. They've got a lovely old Provençal farmhouse near Mougins. Always full of strays, cats, people, dogs, a couple of horses. Very kind. Your father was there two years ago, just after the war ended. They only just moved in for good this year. Gave up their flat in London. I was going to try for RADA...."

"What's RADA?" thinking it was something I should know, disguised by his English accent.

"Royal Academy of Dramatic Arts."

"Oh. You want to act?"

He laughed. "I always act."

"No, I mean...."

"Yes, yes, I know," still laughing. "Anyway, instead of RADA I'm at the Conservatoire here. Racine, Molière, and my bloody accent. Not doing very well, I'm afraid. Unless something happens I'll end up playing English butlers in Elvire Popesco comedies for the rest of my life. But that's neither here nor there."

He got up and looked around the room, blinking despondently at the mess of baggage, the piles of clothes half

12

in and half out of bags and trunks. Three suitcases, though small, remained unopened. He looked mournfully at them, then at the window.

"Look, it's such a beautiful day. Why don't you finish this some other time? Let's go out and I'll show you Paris. You can't possibly be tired after a week on the *de Grasse*, after all."

As it turned out it took me several days to get my things in order, because every day was a beautiful day and every day Claude had something else to do rather than "fuss with girdles and twinsets", as he put it.

Paris was an incredible world to live in, in 1948. Claude knew everyone. Within days I was at home in the cafés, the little restaurants, the bars, within weeks I knew half the Left Bank. We wandered through those first weeks, Claude and I, he carelessly, naturally, his own domain, I dreamlike, through the looking-glass. I wrote ecstatic letters to Tor to which he replied just as enthusiastically, adding only occasionally a brief paternal line of warning about going overboard. Paternalism was not Tor's strong point; it never quite rang true.

Whom did I know in those early days? American jazz musicians who had begun to flock to Paris, mostly Negroes, supplying the Left Bank with some of the most exciting jazz in Europe at the time, a wonderful warm group of young painters at the Grande Chaumière, mostly American again, and a few Spaniards or Catalans, painters too. Then the Saint-Germain-des-Prés crowd who were Claude's friends. French actors, directors, camera-men, boys at the school of cinematography, all of them young, all of them beginning, all of them full of the contagious energy of the post-war years. Then there were others. We knew Adamov, we listened to Greco, just beginning too, we read Sartre and Camus, de Beauvoir and Prévert, we crowded into the *cinémathèque*, into the little theatres, the Rose Rouge, the Tabou, had endless conversations at the Flore or the Montana.

That was the beginning. The beginning was Claude. The beginning was my own awakening into a world of enthusiasm, into a period of grace, before things went sour again in the fifties. The warmth of the late forties in Paris, the upsurge of activity, the bursting of energies hoarded during the war, the absence of *arrivisme*, made Paris into a kind of heaven for youngsters. I know it did not last long, but at the time it looked as though it would go on forever, not only go on but grow into something we all expected from the winning of the war—a brave new world in our image. That did not happen. But the fact that it looked like it was going to happen was the touchstone of the mood of 1948.

That was the beginning, in June. The summer went by full of superlatives, full of amazements. My first glimpse of the Mediterranean, my first visit to Italy. The first time I stood in the Piazza de la Signoria in Florence, feeling God-knows-what choking awareness of beauty, I suddenly remembered Tor's voice and the way he looked as he saw me off on the New York pier. "How I envy you seeing it all for the first time." Standing in Florence in that breathtaking square I knew what he meant.

We ended up in Cannes at Claude's parents' house in early September, brown, tired, broke, having "done Italy like latter-day Jamesians", said Claude. Fred set me up an easel in a spare room and I started to paint for the first time since my arrival. In the three weeks we stayed in the Midi I did four large canvases, a record for me. I am still a very slow painter.

Monique, a tall, classically beautiful woman, cool and composed in that rather mad household, was enormously kind to me. She was about Tor's age, in her early forties. I was struck by her extraordinary grace; her movements seemed coordinated by some kind of magic. I found myself sketching her at table, or on the beach, her arms, her hands, the attitude of her head and shoulders.

One evening she said, "Do you ever see your mother?"

"Yes," I replied, rather surprised. "Of course I do. I used to spend school holidays with them on Long Island. Do you know her?"

"I did know her. A long time ago. She was very lovely." Monique smiled.

"She still is."

"Did she have more children?"

I laughed. "No. I guess I discouraged her. I've always lived with Tor, you know."

She smiled. I could see Claude in her smile. "Yes. I know. What is her husband like?"

"Oh, pleasant enough. He's a scientist. Physics. They are very well suited to each other." Then in a burst of candour, "I'll never understand how she ever married Tor. They're so painfully different!"

Monique laughed. "No wonder you get along so well with your father. You're exactly like him." I smiled at that. People have been telling me that ever since I can remember.

By mid-September we began to think of going back to Paris, to "real life", said Claude. School was to reopen in October but we both wanted to get back and get settled.

Monique and Fred decided to come up to Paris for a while, too. We drove, taking three days for a trip than can be done in twelve hours. If I had fallen in love with Paris when I first arrived, I fell even further for the countryside in those three days. More so than with Italy. The infinite beauty of rural France was a revelation to me.

Chapter Three

SMOOTHLY, in the warm autumn I slipped into a comfortable routine. I went to classes at the Grande Chaumière and took lessons from André Lhote twice a week. For lunch I went to Chez Wadja with other students at the Grande Chaumière, to Chez Wadja or to half a dozen other small, cheap student restaurants like it in Montparnasse.

I met Claude most evenings. He had the use of his mother's apartment, she and Fred were seldom there. It was a big bourgeois flat with large rooms and high ceilings which Monique had inherited from her own parents. It had a great deal of charm, was full of Victorian furniture, amazing *fin-de-siècle* bric-à-brac, opaline lamps and handsome fireplaces in most of the rooms. Claude's friends roamed about the place at all hours. Many of them lived in student lodgings or small hotels or, that famous Paris stand-by, sixth-floor maids' rooms. It was unusual for someone our age to have a huge apartment all to himself. Thus, it was a kind of centre of activity for a substantial part of Saint-Germain-des-Prés. Occasionally I would bring my art school friends to the rue des Saints-Pères—Teddy Klein, Bob Andrews, one or two others, including a handful of Spanish painters who used to go to one of the Montparnasse cafés, the Bar des États-Unis. Generally, however, I would meet Claude in the early evening and we would have dinner with two or three others at the Petit Saint-Benoit or Chez Augustin or the Beaux-Arts, where we would collect a few more strays. Afterwards we would go to the Flore or the Tabou or the Rose Rouge. There was an infinite variety of places to go; it all depended on our pocketbooks. Once in a while I would stay in Mont-parnasse with Teddy and Bob, and spend the evening at the Bar des États-Unis, where Djuri Cortez played the guitar and where we were able to dance. By then my French was passable and I got along marvellously with everyone. I was particularly fond of the Spaniards, most of them painters, all of them good-looking and all wonderful fun.

Looking back now from my anonymous room in the Hotel Cayré on a fading spring afternoon fifteen years later, it is hard to believe that I was that twenty-year-old child in her New-Look skirts, tight wide belts, and turtle-neck sweaters. It is hard to believe that there is nothing left of that child, nothing left of those years, nothing but an ugly scar, crudely healed and only superficially hidden. After fifteen years.

I must come to terms now. I cannot go back to London tomorrow without finding out, without an attempt at finding out. I must get out of this room and go down in the lift, walk to Vavin and the Select. I will not do any more than that; the walk, the drink at the Select will be my attempt. I will not look through the telephone book for names that are probably not there. I will only go to the Select. If after all these years I am to find out it will be there, nowhere else.

Slowly, then, I gathered myself together, dressing with deliberate care, watching the reflection of a thirty-five-year-old woman in the mirror, avoiding my own eyes, keeping the panic I had lived with all day at a distance. Keeping thought and reason at a distance. Mechanically, with precision in my gestures, getting dressed to go out into the streets to find out. Hoping I would not find out. Hoping desperately for invisibility, anonymity, in this changed city, hoping that there would be no one in the Select who would have known Mihailo or who would remember me. Throwing away my thick armour, shedding coat after coat of the prickly mail that had protected this part of me all these years, feeling naked and cold as I had felt so long ago in New York, when Tor died and I was alone, shedding all this and the years of protection with Gavin in that other life, I closed the door behind me and walked onto the Boulevard Raspail, fifteen years later, thirteen years too late to begin my search for Mihailo.

Chapter Four

Aᴺᴰ so it was. I walked up the Boulevard Raspail alone. It was as though I were beginning to learn to walk all over again. As though I were emerging from a long paralysis. As I walked the movements became more natural, the street grew safer under my legs. I kept a tight balance in my movements, picking my way through the minutes carefully, as I had done through the years, before. Slowly, I began to breathe more normally, slowly I began to relax.

Paris is a most unghostlike ghost town. It is almost impossible to look at it, even under these curious circumstances, without a certain affection. Have the streets changed? The houses seem cleaner. Of course, Malraux's campaign for brightening up the buildings. Of course. It is no longer uniformly grey, that rather wonderful grey of 1948. This street. I will cut through on this street. Chez Adrien. It is still there. Late at night when the Coupole, the Select had closed we would go to Chez Adrien for a last beer. A crowd of us from the Grande Chaumière. I wonder whether young painters from the art schools nearby still go to Chez Adrien. The pictures outside the door. It looks sleeker, more prosperous now.

I must look strange, the doorman glanced at me oddly.

And the Select. Bits and shreds of the coats of mail at my feet, standing in front of . . . of what? A large, noisy café? A café like hundreds of others? Like hundreds of others, perhaps, but unlike them because this is Paris and because people say the Select is unchanged, the same Yugoslavs, the same painters as before. But would they be likely to know?

19

Would he be likely to be here, a thirty-seven-year-old man now, someone I do not know, embarrassed by me after all these years. Embarrassed by a ghost from a faraway past, to whom he owes an apology.

No, there is no more Mihailo here. There is nothing left of 1948 here. There are only strangers in a café called the Select. I can go in.

I hesitated. Didn't Claude meet Alexis here? Yes. But that was in 1950. Not now. No one is left now. No one that matters. I must believe that. I must finally come to understand that. I must know once and for all that Paris is not a threat to me, that there is no Mihailo any more. Nor am I the same. I am a thirty-five-year-old woman, the mother of four sons. I am well-dressed and have grey in my hair. I am no longer a twenty-year-old art student in a long New-Look skirt wearing my hair long and straight down my back, wearing a paint-splotched trench coat, wearing Capezio ballerinas. I am Mrs. Gavin Davies from London, a Sunday painter, and in the Select of 1963 I am invisible. Confident in my invisibility I entered the Select and sat down at a terrace table. I ordered a Pernod.

Gavin has been right all along. This self-imposed exile from France, from Paris is senseless. I looked around the other tables, a heady confidence growing within me, the confidence of a new swimmer. One or two people looked familiar. But were they really? Wasn't it rather that they looked like their counterparts in Chelsea or Greenwich Village? The big, floppy sweaters, the beards, the slight touch of grime. All that is an interchangeable uniform. They were not familiar because I had recognised their faces, they were familiar as types. The international brotherhood of café dwellers. I relaxed, reached out and poured water into the Pernod and sipped it calmly, the new confidence stronger than the alcohol. How long ago.

But what if it were Alexis who came in the door? Not Mihailo but Alexis. Thin, tall Alexis with his hawk-like nose, his burning eyes behind thick-lensed glasses, Alexis with his curious walk and his long sensitive hands. Alexis with his passionate love for Mihailo, his cold dislike of me. God-fearing Alexis, ungiving, unbending, the fire of dry ice in his eyes as he judged me. What would I say if Alexis walked through the door now and joined that table of Serbs in the corner? Now.

My head throbbed, my throat grew dry. I have never feared anyone, I have never hated anyone except Alexis. For all these years, all this time I have never once altered in my fear of him and in my hatred of him. He alone is responsible, he alone is answerable; whatever he did to change Mihailo's mind, to turn him away from me, was done deliberately in cold calculation. He knew I loved Mihailo and he must have known Mihailo loved me, but that was not enough. He mistrusted such love, dismissed it and when his chance came he took it.

Yet is that true? Is that what happened? What could Alexis have used as a weapon? Why must I be tortured like this? All the confidence, all the new strength drained away in the unavoidable awareness of my own pain, my undiminished weakness before Alexis, before reality. Panic-stricken again, I tried to summon the courage to call to the waiter. Yet fear gripped at my throat as though the whole café would turn and stare at me if I were to use my voice—stare and recognise me. Know that I was here searching for Mihailo, come back to claim him, who had no right to him. I groped in my bag for a franc note large enough to cover several times over the price of a Pernod and left the café.

Shakily, on the Boulevard Montparnasse, no longer tear-less, no longer numb, Mihailo's face clear to me, his hand in mine, the knowledge of his tall young body by my side, I realised that for thirteen years I have kept him within me, a part of me, a private sorrow, a private joy, a corner within me which was a hope, a buoy, and for thirteen years I have kept this love alive while pretending to have buried it, released myself from it for another stability. All these years are now undone. As though they had never happened. And I am rendered as raw and exposed as I was in the very beginning.

In March 1950 I flew home to New York to find Tor in a small Connecticut hospital, unrecognisable in relentless pain. For fifteen weeks he lingered on, fifteen weeks of horror, dying before my eyes. We were alone, this different, wraith-like Tor who had been surrounded all his life by laughter and youth, forty-four years old, his long yellow hair on a hospital pillow, myself lost and uncomprehending by his side. All the letters I wrote to Mihailo were returned, one by one, like ghosts themselves. I wrote Claude in London to find him, to find out what was the matter. And all the time Tor was dying piece by piece. I had never known pain, never known death, never known fear, and all at once I knew only death and fear and pain. Claude wrote that he couldn't find Mihailo, he seemed to have deliberately disappeared; an embarrassed letter.

Then the hideous world I walked into on the day Tor died, the empty world of no Tor, no love, no Mihailo, the world of adults for which I was so unprepared, of no money, of hostile relatives, of unrelenting medical bills, doctors and undertakers and finally, my mother, that patient stranger taking over the ragged edges. And in dying Tor swept every-thing along with him, the world as I had known it, the structure of love as I had understood it, the basis of life as I had believed in it. I walked out of that world in to a cold reality as though I had been born at the age of twenty-two.

But before that birth I was to slip into what I suppose could be called near insanity.

My mother insisted that I go and stay with her on Long Island after it was all over. It was only natural, I suppose. But as the days passed the reality of her house, her husband, her voice, her life became more and more confused to me. I found it hard to talk in her presence, I found it hard to eat, to focus on her voice, to hear what she said. During the warm days I walked along the beaches, sat on the dunes watching the water lick hungrily at the sands. The sea became a comfort, the only presence I could bear to have near to me. Cold water tugging at my feet on the shore, waves splashing, pulling me, the ocean's weight became my weight.

It wasn't hard to disappear. In fact it was amazingly easy. I told her I was leaving for the weekend to stay with a girl who had been a childhood friend. She was very pleased with me and asked me to phone her when I arrived.

I packed a small bag and left. It had been an effort to lie to her; not that the lie meant anything to me in itself. It was merely difficult to gather the energy needed to think of the lie, and once having thought it out, to mouth it into words and to put the words into action. A terrible effort. I looked at a map in the Manhattan bus terminal and found the place that seemed best suited to what I had had in mind. It was a small town in Maryland. It was on a bay. I had never been there; I had never known anyone who had ever been there. There was nothing to connect me with the town. They would have a hard time tracing me there. And the bus ticket only cost six dollars.

It was dusk when I arrived in the town. The days were long. It did not get dark till ten p.m. I went into the first drug store I came to and ate a sandwich and a malted milk. The man behind the counter spoke with a southern accent. I noticed that. It came as a surprise; I was probably in the South though I hadn't thought of that. The town was pretty. It had large white houses on tree-lined streets. It was different from New England but very pretty. There was a small bay with many pleasure boats at anchor. Not big yachts, small ones that might sleep four or six. Several wide avenues led from the harbour to the centre of the town. I chose one of them at random and began walking.

Within a few minutes I noticed a white frame house set far back on a sloping lawn. On the front gate was a neat little sign reading: "Rooms for rent". I walked up the driveway and knocked at the door. A middle-aged woman answered. I told her I was looking for a room. She asked me for how long. But I was prepared for that and I answered calmly, for the summer vacation. That seemed acceptable to her. She showed me upstairs. It was a big room with a small bed and furniture painted white. It looked over the garden which was well kept and scented. I paid ten dollars a week for the room and breakfast, in advance. She left and I fell asleep without undressing.

Within a few days I realised that I would have to find a job. I wanted a job where I would not have to talk to people. That, too, was easy. The new supermarket hired me. I spent the day hitting the keys of an adding machine, totalling up peoples' grocery bills, taking their money and giving them change. I seldom had to say more than the amount of their bills and thank you. The other people who worked with me were pleasant and uninquisitive. The difference in our accents seemed to mark a line between us. Once a girl asked me why I had come to the town. I told her a lie about having friends nearby. No one else asked again.

Within a short time I had established a routine. I rose early and went to work. When the supermarket closed I ate my dinner at one of the soda-fountains. There were two movie-houses in the town. They changed their programmes twice a week. Thus, four times a week I went to the movies. Then I went home and slept. On the other three nights I went for walks in the countryside around the town or by the beaches. Occasionally people would try to talk to me; boys or men would try to follow me. I would hurry my step and out-distance them quickly. It made me uncomfortable and I was much happier in the movies. Soon I stopped taking walks altogether. I returned to my room, washed and ironed my few clothes and went off to sleep. I was capable of sleeping twelve hours a night.

The weeks passed. I had no idea of how long I had been there when a man came to the supermarket and asked for me. As soon as I heard his accent I knew he must be someone come to fetch me back. He seemed surprised that I made no move to resist him. I left my little cubbyhole without a protest, took off the white apron I wore and walked out of the store with him. He tried to talk to me on the way to the house where I lived. He talked about how worried my mother was. I did not believe that "worried" was the right word but I didn't say anything. I packed my small bag, said goodbye to the landlady and got into his car with him. We drove to New York but I slept all the way.

My mother was kind and tactful, so was her husband. I agreed to see a psychiatrist but refused to go to a nursing home. She seemed satisfied. It was still hot and I resumed the long walks I had taken before. It must have been September, for the beaches were only crowded on weekends. I stayed home on weekends.

The doctor was a huge Saint Bernard of a man. Hair grew out of his ears and nose. I felt nothing towards him, neither hostility nor affection nor even reticence. At first. At first we only spoke about my childhood. I could talk of Tor in terms of my childhood but that was all.

I went to see the doctor every day at eleven. He lived a

few towns away on the Long Island Railroad. Sometimes I walked back. It was a two-hour walk and part of it went over the dunes near the sea, I told him that and he scowled.

"You shouldn't wander around the lonely dunes, not even in the middle of the day, It could be dangerous."

I don't know why, but that angered me. It was the first thing to touch me enough to arouse anger since Tor died. I rose from the couch and started to berate him, call him a hairy old fool, a stupid blundering ass. He stared at me, shocked, his eyes wide open. Then something catlike crawled into his expression and I noticed it. It quelled my anger immediately. I could see that he thought he had found something. I sat down and apologised; confused, shaking, but on my guard. When I looked at him again the cat had disappeared and I hesitated. Perhaps I had only imagined it. For the first time I was afraid of him. I could see that he was going to win.

That winter—I think it was in February—they found me a job. I worked in a public library. I saw the doctor at seven in the evening. The nights were long, cold, the winds biting. I was no longer able to walk over the dunes. My mother and her husband were infinitely patient with me but never over-indulgent. I was not allowed to miss a session with the analyst. After a certain time I was also expected to meet their guests. Mother insisted. At first I was terrified but soon I became wily about avoiding questions, diverting curiosity, channelling conversations away from myself. Sometimes I would catch my mother looking at me. Was it anger in her eyes, or was it pity? Long after, years after, I realised that it was neither; only sorrow.

Thus, despite the doctor, despite my mother and her husband I learned to build a thick covering around myself. I built it carefully and scientifically and in the teeth of all those who were trying so tactfully to do the opposite. After a bit

I talked to the doctor about Paris and about a boy whose name I would not pronounce—until it finally became too silly and I called him Michel, and the doctor breathed a little sigh of satisfaction and I another one of even greater satisfaction. I talked about Tor's death and my strange flight to the town in Maryland. I found it strange, too, as though it had not really happened to me. I did not mind talking about it. It kept the doctor off Paris. I also talked a great deal about Claude. The doctor kept hinting that I was in love with him. I was becoming crafty at the game and let him think so for a while but in the end I tired of it and we dropped Claude.

That summer I surprised everyone by asking to be permitted to work in a children's camp further out on the island. They all took it as a sign of great progress. I suppose it was. For some time I had realised that I was particularly comfortable with children. There were no devious games to be played with them, no exhausting conversations to ride, nothing demanded of me more than an interest in them. I welcomed the release, the freedom from myself, freedom from the concern of the doctor and my mother's anxious eyes, freedom from everything that had to do with me. It was another flight, but a healthier one and I enjoyed it.

That was how freedom, if indeed that is the word, that was how it came. Little by little, almost imperceptibly, one small gain at a time. I returned from the summer healthy in body and relaxed of mind. I spoke of taking a more interesting job. The way my mother leaped at any constructive suggestion I made had an unfortunately negative effect upon me. Petulantly, like an unpleasant child, I was moved to do just the opposite of what I had originally suggested just to irritate her. Curious reversal to the womb, curious spiky womb. The hours with the analyst dragged on through the winter and my withdrawal deepened. My mother never lost her patience though God knows she had ample reason to.

One bright December afternoon, the sky an electric blue, a cold yellow sun casting giant shadows on the suburban garden hedge, suddenly I began to cry. To cry as I had not done in many months; to cry and pour out all the pain and numbness, to cry and scream alone in that jarring light, that bright implacable light, till my eyes were swollen and red and my face burned from the wet cold. Hysterical tears washing down to the front of my coat, knotting my hair; child's tears releasing the dense withdrawal till I was brought back to the reaches of feeling, of human contact, out of the whirlpool of unreasoned despair. And then it was over.

I stopped seeing the analyst. I moved from my mother's house into a small apartment in the city. I got a job. In time I met Gavin and with him, thanks to him, moved from that half-world of my own making to this other that I inhabit still.

Through the years I have searched for an explanation of why Mihailo left me, an explanation of why he disappeared, but in not finding, in my vain search, I learned to accept not finding; I learned that sometimes there are no answers. Yet now I find that the lesson, like so many others, was false. Once again I am stripped bare, once again I must begin all over. Begin the search for Mihailo.

Chapter Five

ROSSELLINI and Magnani were the big noise in 1948. The queues for Open City were endless. I decided to wait till the queue got good and long, say ten minutes before show time, and then I'd trot off to the Ursulines and see if someone I knew was in the queue. It was a good system and generally worked. Even if it turned out that I didn't know anyone there I could always ask someone to buy my ticket for me. Anyway, it was worth a try.

I had dinner alone at the Petit Saint-Benoit that night and toward nine thirty strolled over toward the Latin Quarter, cutting through on the rue Monsieur-le-Prince. It was a cold November evening, a Paris cold, damp and rather luminous. I remember the walk, the light on the boulevard, the pockets of fog. Two boys I knew were going into the Prince Pol on the rue Monsieur-le-Prince as I was passing by. They stopped me and asked me to go in with them, someone or other was going to play the guitar. I hesitated for a minute but decided in favour of Rossellini and kept on going. But the queue at the Ursulines came as a disappointment. Not only did I not recognise anyone, but the average age of the people seemed to be over sixty. It was unheard of at a Latin Quarter cinema: no one from Montparnasse, no one from Saint-Germain-des-Prés. On the contrary, they looked like a delegation of apartment owners from Neuilly.

Then I saw the boy. He was way up on the line, standing in the doorway. Probably had been waiting for an hour to be that far ahead. I did not recognise him from any of the Left Bank cafés, but he was about my age. He was reading a book.

I looked down the queue again, just to make sure, then I decided that he would have to be "it".

"Pardon, monsieur," I began in a low voice, and he jumped. He looked so startled that I laughed, at which he looked even more startled. "Je m'excuse, mais puis-je vous demander de m'acheter un billet?"

I kept my voice as low as possible so that the others wouldn't object. People who have been standing on line for an hour have a tendency to take a dim view of bright young things who come along five minutes before the film, flapping their eyelashes. . . .

"Mais, je suis confus, mademoiselle, je ne crois pas que j'ai assez d'argent sur moi . . ."

And I laughed again. "No, you don't understand. I'll pay my own way, it's just that the queue is too long." He looked visibly surprised to see so many people behind him. "Tiens."

"Oh, yes. Of course. Gladly," he said. And then he smiled. I had never seen a smile like his, not in a grown man anyway. It seemed to have all the candour, all the innocence, all the light of a child.

Since my arrival in Paris I had met scores of young people through Claude and his friends. The general atmosphere of the Left Bank in 1948 was conducive to such ease. People talked to one another, there was a vibrant café life, my own contemporaries were open, eager for new ideas, new people. Yet, in this tall boy at the door of the Ursulines I was, instantly aware of something different.

The line moved and we went into the cinema. He hesitated as we walked down the aisle.

"Sit with me," I blurted out impulsively. "This is a film one shouldn't see alone."

He looked at me a bit curiously, seemed to weigh what I had said, then agreed, somewhat like a serious child. He was very handsome, I noticed, in a severe kind of way. He started to move into a place near the rear, but I took his hand and urged him on down to the front, the seventh or eighth row.

"But it's too close," he protested.

"Oh, no!" I corrected knowledgeably. "You have to sit up close otherwise you miss things."

His hand tightly gripped in mine, we moved into our seats. We kept our coats on in 1948 because nothing was heated. Sitting back waiting for Rossellini, deep in our seats, I looked at him and smiled. He was timid, or, more likely, I had intimidated him. I dug into my pockets and brought out an American chocolate bar, slightly squashed by the weight of cigarettes, matches and other bric-à-brac. He looked at it.

"Are you American?" he asked in English.

"Yes. My chocolates give me away?"

"No. Your manners."

I laughed. "Doesn't everyone talk to you in cinema queues and drag you down to the first rows?"

We both laughed. "Are you a student?" he asked, disengaging the paper from the chocolate, trying to keep his fingers from getting sticky.

"Art," I answered, fishing in the other pocket for a Kleenex. I gave it to him. He looked at it with curiosity.

"What is this?"

"To wipe your fingers. They're all chocolatey. It's a paper handkerchief, Kleenex."

"Aha," he said, taking it carefully in his clean left hand. "How clever."

"You've never seen a paper handkerchief?" I asked.

"No. I don't know any Americans. Does everyone have paper handkerchiefs and chocolate in their pockets? Do they all talk to other people the way you do?" And he smiled at me very gently, very shyly.

"Not all of them talk as much as I do, but we all have Kleenex." I was grinning at him but instantly I regretted my flipness; it was out of place. No; more than that, rather as though we were speaking two different languages. He looked at me seriously, his very dark eyes in search of a meaning other than a joke. But realising that I was joking, he laughed too. He was dressed in an army trench coat and wore a thick navy blue turtle-neck sweater and a pair of nondescript trousers.

"My name is Mihailo Kerovitch. I am studying at the Orthodox Theological Seminary, to be a priest."

The lights of the cinema snapped off and the newsreel began just in time to mask my surprise. Yet all during the film my mind kept coming back to it, with a twinge of inexplicable confusion. A priest, an Orthodox priest. Good heavens.

We left the cinema together, talking enthusiastically about Rossellini, about the new concept of films in Italy, and finally about the war. He had been in the mountains with the Chetniks, he told me, then in a series of German prison camps.

"How old are you?" I asked.

"Nearly twenty-two."

"But you were very young to have been in the war."

"Oh, so was everyone else," he answered, shrugging his shoulders.

We walked along the Boulevard Saint-Michel to the Seine without saying much. "Shall I take you to your home?" he asked. I looked at the clock at Place Saint-Michel. It was twelve forty-five.

"Oh, you've missed your métro. Where is the Russian Seminary?"

"Quite far. Near the canals. But don't worry about the métro. I can walk home. It wouldn't be the first time, you know."

"Yes, but it's my fault. I should have noticed. You see, I live near here, on the rue du Dragon. I'm so used to being within walking distance of everything that I'd forgotten."

"No. I assure you. It is nothing. I often walk home."

"Don't you have to be in at a certain time in your seminary?" I asked. It was difficult for me to talk to him when I let myself think of him as a priest; as though it caused me embarrassment.

"Yes, but not on weekends. On weekends I am free. Oh, even on other days I can come in late, too. It is not serious. The bishop, if he knows, would scold me, but that is all. Scold? You say scold, don't you?"

"Yes, scold." His serious expression made me smile, but to myself. "Where did you learn English?"

"As a child. But I have forgotten it. I get it mixed up with French now. My mother teaches English. She has even translated poetry from the English into Bulgarian. Donne, Blake, Burns. But he was a Scot, wasn't he? And Yeats. She also translated Yeats."

"Mihailo means Michael, doesn't it?"

"Yes."

"It's somehow stronger than Michael."

He laughed. "Is it? And Carola is like Christmas carols. Adeste Fideles?"

"Yes," and we both laughed.

"Do you have many friends in Paris?"

"No. Not many. And you?"

"Yes, lots. My father lived here before the war, in bits and pieces, and he knows everyone. Also in bits and pieces. He teaches English at a small college near New York. Where all the girls fall in love with him. He's only forty-two and quite fabulous-looking."

"Forty-two! He married very young. And your mother is also so young?"

"They are the same age. But they are divorced. I live, that is, I always have lived with my father."

He looked at me quickly, his eyes wide with amazement. "Not with your mother?"

Of course, I was used to people being surprised by the fact that Tor had received custody of his five-year-old daughter, surprise tinged with amusement if the people knew Tor or my mother. But Mihailo looked scandalised!

"Actually," I explained, "my mother was far less attached to me than my father. Then they both had to work—it was during the depression in America—and Tor could afford me more than my mother could. Well, that was the official version, anyway." I turned my head to look at him. We were under a street lamp, his face was very clear to me. His brown eyes, under a faint frown, looked at me with curiosity.

"Don't misunderstand." I said to him, smiling. "I had a very happy childhood."

"One gets a strange idea of America from books and from movies, you know. Divorce. I think you are the first person I have ever met who has divorced parents. My father is a priest, my grandfather was a priest. America is . . . what can one say? . . . far removed. . . . "

I did not have time to answer. We had reached the corner of the Boulevard Saint-Germain. A group of people were coming out of a doorway and I recognised Claude among them.

"Hello," he called out. "Come to the Flore for a nightcap."

Mihailo hesitated. "Your friends?" he asked, looking after them.

"Yes. Claude Gallien. He's my closest friend here, my guardian angel. Come along and I'll introduce you."

"But it is very late. . . . I would not like to intrude on your friends," he said flatly.

"Intrude? At the Flore?" I laughed. "Come on. You'll enjoy them."

"No, really . . . I mean . . . I don't think I have enough . . ."

I suddenly saw why. "Let me invite you. After all, you were good enough to get me into the Ursulines. And besides, next time will be your turn."

He looked horrified.

"You know how it is with students," I continued, pretending not to see his embarrassment, "the one who has pays. Not like that with budding priests?"

"With what?"

"Embryo bishops?"

He looked even more horrified for a second, but seeing my smile he suddenly began to laugh at what was obviously a bit of blasphemy in his book. "I begin to think the films and novels do not exaggerate."

Claude and the others had taken a table toward the rear. Claude was facing the door as we entered. He grinned at me and I saw his eyes move to Mihailo, examining him swiftly, almost coldly. We sat down and joined the others. I watched Mihailo sitting near me. Tall, large-framed but thin, very thin, fine brown eyes, a good brow, delicate bone structure along the cheeks, a soft mouth, rather stubborn chin, square strong hands nervously fingering his frayed raincoat sleeves. The quality of innocence in his face, which I did not mistake despite my own innocence, was disarming.

He did not talk much, but around café tables there is always enough talk going on. No one noticed him. Except me.

Around one thirty we began to pay attention to the waiters, who were making closing noises round us. It was time to go. Someone suggested going to Les Halles for fried potatoes and sausages. Mihailo looked at me, dismayed.

"Are you tired?" he asked.

"No."

35

"Neither am I."

"Are you hungry?"

"No . . . no, not really . . ."

But I saw he was. All of a sudden I saw that the fine cheek-bones, the beautiful planes of his face were due to being hungry more than to being Slav. Why didn't I realise it before? Idiot! He probably had eaten lentil soup at some student canteen, and that a good eight hours ago. How stupid of me not to have guessed.

"Well, I'm hungry," I said, and moved toward the door with the others. "Come on. The frites are great at a little stand we know."

Philippe, one of Claude's buddies, had a pre-war Citroen. We all crowded into it as best we could. There were seven of us. Mihailo and I sat in the back with Claude, and a tiny, thin girl, whom we called Pretzel, was inched onto Claude's lap. From her perch she peered over at Mihailo and groaned.

"Oooh, who's that? He's gorgeous."

"Shh," I whispered, "he hates girls."

"Oh, not another one," moaned the Pretzel. "Why are they always the prettiest?" She leaned back on Claude, who was eyeing me curiously.

Armed with paper cones of *frites* and spicy North African sausages in huge pieces of *baguette*, we sat on the steps of Saint-Eustache until it began to rain. Home, decided the owner of the car, and everyone seemed to agree with him, except me.

"I have a cousin who is staying in Paris for a while. He lives near here. I will go to his room tonight instead of the seminary. Tomorrow is Saturday. There are no classes."

"Oh, good. You won't have to walk home."

"And you. Your friends live near you, I suppose?" he asked. We were standing slightly to the left of the others, apart.

36

"Yes. Claude lives on the next street, rue des Saints-Pères. Philippe lives just over the Flore in a maid's room and Pretzel, well, I don't know that she lives anywhere, really. Philippe is the proprieter of our elegant car, by the way. He's studying at IDHEC."

"What is IDHEC?"

"The school of cinematography," I said, surprised that anyone would not know what IDHEC was.

"He wants to be an actor?" Mihailo asked, turning his gaze on Philippe.

"No," I laughed, "a director. If he wanted to be an actor he would be at the Conservatoire. Like Claude."

"Claude is at the Conservatoire? Oh. And the others?"

"I really don't know them, the others."

"And Pretzel, as you call her?"

"She's studying to be a tart, I think. . . . "

"A tart? Is not that a kind of cake? What is a tart?" and his serious expression made me laugh even more.

"Don't laugh at me, you make me feel silly."

"No, no. I'm sorry, but a tart is . . ."

"Yes, I see. I see now what a tart is. Not a cake." And we both laughed.

Then there was a silence between us. I looked at his very fine eyes and was aware of how painfully out of place he must have felt. A theology student at the Russian Seminary.

"Mihailo. . . . " His eyes were on mine. "Tomorrow could you come and have lunch with me?"

"Oh . . . "

"Please. I'd like it so much."

"Well, I . . . "

"Thirty, rue du Dragon, fourth floor right, chez Madame Ferson. Around one."

"Merci," he smiled. And again I was struck by that extra-ordinary light.

37

Claude shouted from the waiting car. We stood on the pavement in front of Saint-Eustache and I said good night, feeling the colour rising in my cheeks, hoping he would not notice as we shook hands like two serious children.

Chapter Six

THE next day I bought the biggest steak I could find, an enormous loaf of bread, a huge lump of paté, my ration of milk—because I was under twenty-one I was allowed a pint of milk a day—and a giant *pain d'épice*, that rubbery French gingerbread which was a staple in those days. I puttered around with a rice pilaff, a healthy salad with two hard-boiled eggs chopped up in it, and a bottle of wine.

Madame Ferson was amazed at my preparations. It was the first meal I had ever cooked in her kitchen. Up to then I had lived on a steady diet of ham sandwiches or else eaten in restaurants. I was terribly excited by it all, took ages in the bath, ironed a white blouse with infinite care and decanted the bottle of *vin ordinaire* as it if were the finest burgundy. I was sure he would be on time. At one o'clock I was all ready. The table was ready, too, with a white table cloth which the bemused landlady had donated to the festivities. The rice was ready, the steak all set to go under the grill, the salad prepared, everything all set.

But he was not on time. By one thirty I began to think there might have been a misunderstanding. By two I knew he would not come. By two thirty I was in tears. The table, the steak, the rice stared at me stupidly. Madame Ferson's padding feet in the hall, discreetly avoiding my door, made me feel the biggest fool in Paris.

I lay back on my bed, putting wrinkles in the well-ironed blouse, smoking cigarette after cigarette, refusing to acknowledge anything deeper than anger, refusing to see the gaping disappointment. At five I went out, avoiding Madame Ferson, and spent the evening with Claude and Philippe. Neither mentioned Mihailo.

There was no more news of him. He did not call or write to apologise. He just disappeared. I thought of him, not in anger but with a kind of sadness. How beautiful he was to look at; not handsome, no, but beautiful, a curious light in his face that accented his eyes and mouth. Why did he not come that Saturday? Why?

The following Saturday was a magnificent autumn day, cold but bright and clear, the sky a crisp blue. Claude woke me at nine, not by his usual telephone call but by barging into my bedroom, Madame Ferson hot on his heels, scolding him from under her curlers. He offered her a Louis Jouvet bow, asked her if she would like a cocktail, waited for her to register the proper dismay and leave. It was a routine performance which both seemed to enjoy.

"Let's go to Père Lachaise and put a posy on de Nerval's grave," he said, surveying me as I got out of bed. "Come on, get yourself into one of your togas and walking-shoes and on this beautiful day we will render homage to ce gentil Gérard, the spiritual father of us all."

In the five months that I had been in Paris I had rendered homage to "ce gentil Gérard de Nerval" six times.

"Can't we visit Baudelaire? He's closer." I was sleepy.

"The Prince of Night on a day like this? Ugh. No. Not Baudelaire. La Dame aux Camélias perhaps, and in passing a brief hello to cher Oscar of the green carnation and then a few anemones scattered over sleeping de Nerval..."

"You're a ghoul, you know. Recite me something from Sylvie while I dress. And don't look."

"I won't look. Besides, virgins are only interesting in the abstract. In practice I'll leave you to someone more clinically inclined and dig you next year."

"Pig. Anyway, what makes you so sure I'm a virgin?"

"My sweet little Carola. You reek of virginity."

"Oh?"

"Now, don't be miffed. It's really quite touching."

He laughed and proceeded to be "English" for several minutes of Wilde, Chesterton and a pastiche of Ronald Firbank, until I drowned his voice by running the tap water full blast.

We did go to Père Lachaise and we did put a small bouquet of anemones on Gérard de Nerval's grave. We did nod to Oscar Wilde, Marguerite Gautier, Chopin, and that spiritualist man whose grave is always surrounded by drab old ladies deep in communion with his ghost.

But by then my mind was no longer on de Nerval and his colleagues at Père Lachaise. I had just noticed on my map of Paris that the canals Mihailo had spoken of were quite close by. If I walked straight north I would come to them. The Russian Seminary was marked on the map. Not more than fifteen minutes away, I calculated.

On an impulse I turned to Claude and lied, "Listen, since I'm here I think I'll call on a friend of Tor's who lives near here."

He blinked. "Now?" I realised immediately that my lie was transparent. "Tor has friends in Belleville? How odd." But Claude was kind enough not to push it any further. He took my arm. "First let's have lunch at La Villette. You haven't been there yet. It's the quarter by the abattoirs. Most amazing steaks and joints. You would think it was Chicago."

I felt perfectly silly. What a stupid idea that was; why should I go wandering around the canals thinking vaguely about someone I hardly knew? Claude's familiar face peered at me.

"What are you up to?" he asked.

"Nothing."

"Well, then, to the steaks we go."

And we did. At one point Claude looked up from his preoccupation with his meal and asked casually, oh so casually, "By the way, what ever happened to that boy? You know, the thin one at the Flore."

"I don't know. Haven't seen him since." I could feel myself colouring and was furious.

"Where did you meet him?"

"In the queue at the Ursulines."

"How intellectual. What does he do?"

"Student."

"What kind?"

"Oh, I don't know. Philosophy or something."

"What is he?"

"What is he?"

"Yes. What is he? Nationality, I mean . . ."

"Some kind of Russian, I think."

"Ah, of course. Red? White?"

"Very white, I have a feeling."

Claude pretended to turn it over in his mind, playing an irritating game with me. "Yes, a Cossack? No, too thin and pale hands. Dostoevski or Mayakov. . ."

"Oh, stop it. You're not funny."

"Carola, Carola," he grinned.

"I'm sorry, but I hate being teased like that." I got up and went to the ladies' room. He had rattled me and I was furious with myself for biting. But when I came back to the table my anger had disappeared. So had Claude. I found a note leaning up against the empty wine bottle along with a five-thousand-franc bill. The note read: "Pay the bill like a good girl. I'll collect the change tomorrow. Bon voyage."

Chapter Seven

THE Russian church is located toward the middle of a long, commercial avenue. I took a cab from the restaurant. The church is in a sort of cul-de-sac. There is a tree-lined path, a steep incline past a caretaker's cottage, and the path continues uphill past a small, dilapidated barracks on the left until, higher still, the church is perched on the crest of the hill, to the right. Leaving the noisy street one would never suspect the existence of such a rural scene. It is a curious unexpected church, wood and brick with Byzantine figures painted on the doors and sides. If it were not for the frescoes it would have looked more like a Bavarian chapel.

There was no one in sight, not in the ugly house I had passed or in the two other little lodges on the sides. The trees were still green. In the bright sunshine the sylvan quality was almost unreal. The church is entered by two short staircases leading up to a wooden porch. I walked up the stairs slowly, admiring the paintings which covered the walls. On the porch I looked around me, down at the trees, over to the small houses, to the pathways here and there, but there was no one about. It was very still in the garden. I opened the door of the church and walked in. It is a lovely chapel. Byzantine saints covered the walls, gold leaf, gold haloes, gold-flecked, elongated faces glittered on all sides. The paintings could not have been old but they were moving. Orthodox churches have a touching warmth, a feeling of sun. There is no austerity here; the saints have dark and melting eyes. God is a golden image.

Mihailo opened the door softly. He stood in the light so that my eyes hurt as I looked at him, a golden figure along with all the others. I felt unsure of myself, a trespasser.

"Hello."

"I saw you come in here. . . . "

"Yes."

We both fumbled for words. There seemed nothing more to say.

"Is this where you live?"

"Over there," he answered, pointing to the ugly building I had passed, but not taking his eyes off me. He waited.

"Why didn't you come to lunch that day?" I asked quietly, yet surprised that I should ask at all, as though my voice were talking by itself.

"I . . . I did not think you really . . . I mean, I was not sure . . . "

"Oh."

"Did you wait for me?" His voice was low, unsure.

"Yes, I bought a big steak," but I was sorry I said it because he looked even more unhappy.

"Don't worry about it. Claude and Pretzel helped me eat it," I lied. "It's a very pretty church, isn't it?" I said, moving down toward the altar which didn't look like an altar. "Is that the choir loft?"

"No, the choir is down here, on the right. Up there is for the jeune filles. Like you," he said, and smiled timidly. "You have never been here before?"

"No. I'm not Orthodox," I laughed. "I'm not much of anything."

"Oh, surely you are something!"

"Why surely?" I teased.

"Well, you must believe in something. In God, I mean, in some way." He looked at me, worried.

"Are you going to be a missionary?" I laughed.

44

We walked out of the church together. On the porch I looked out over the hilly path, the tall trees.

"Tell me," breaking the silence, "are you learning your catechism this afternoon or can you come for a walk?"

He laughed at me. "You have such a funny way of talking. Perhaps you need a missionary."

We walked down the steps and crossed the grassy grounds to the main path. "I'll wait for you at the café on the corner, just in case your bearded bishops object to kidnappings."

He went in to the unpainted barracks, and I looked at the dirty windows, the unwashed curtains hanging limply from pieces of string, and at the staircase within, as unpainted as the rest and uninviting. I wondered whether the Catholics, Jews, and Protestants in France were as unhygienic about their future shepherds as the Orthodox.

The bar on the corner was a cheerful little place, as irreverently French as the seminary grounds were Byzantine. One wall was papered with picture postcards.

I ordered a beer and drank it looking at the cards.

It was almost half an hour before Mihailo finally arrived, a little out of breath at that.

"Do you know the canals here?" he asked enthusiastically. "They are very beautiful. You would think you were in Germany or Flanders or a city on the Baltic. They are like nothing in the rest of Paris. Even the street names are different —rue du Rhin, rue de Colmar, rue de Lorraine, pointing eastward. Would you like to walk there?"

He was very much taller than I as we walked along. Through the grey streets, grey despite the sun, hilly broken streets with sharp elbows, up to the canals.

"Why do you want to be a priest?" I asked him.

"Well, I think I told you my father is a priest—you know, of course, that Orthodox priests can marry? Ah, because the French always forget and look shocked when I say my father

45

is a priest. Anyway, I have always been . . . that is, I started studying when I was a small boy. It has always been understood that way."

"You mean you did not choose? Your parents decided for you?"

"No. Not at all like that. For instance. None of my brothers wanted to; they showed no inclination, no vocation, if you like. It was always me."

"Are your parents still alive?" I asked.

"Yes, thank God." He turned to me and smiled. "They are still married, too."

"And your brothers? Are they here in Paris?"

"No. I am the only refugee, the only one here."

"Where does your family live?" I asked.

"In Macedonia. Yugoslavia, that is."

"But you are a Yugoslav, then?"

"In a way. My mother is Bulgarian, my father Russian. I was born in Sofia and lived there as a child, then we went to Belgrade. According to my papers here in France I am a Bulgarian refugee though I haven't seen Bulgaria since 1935. Anyway, my parents are in Yugoslavia and I was in the Yugoslav army or rather with the Chetniks. And I count in Serbian."

He laughed. "When the Americans invented the term 'displaced person' they had me in mind." He said it without rancour, as though it still surprised him. "One of my brothers was very political-minded. He was violently anti-Communist. My father, who is never violently anti-anything, looked at him one evening and said very seriously, 'Ivan, you seem to ignore that you are a direct result of, a primary product of the October Revolution.' Ivan looked at him in astonishment. 'What do you mean, sir?' he asked, shocked. My father did not smile but kept looking at Ivan—he's the eldest—for some seconds. Finally he laughed and said, 'If there had been no

46

revolution I would have stayed quietly home in St. Petersburg like everyone else and not gone off to the wilds of Bulgaria and there would never have been you four young Russo-Bulgarian-Serbs today in Belgrade!' So you see, I've been aware for a long time of being a salade russe."

How different we are, I thought, and yet how different he was from the dozens of other Central Europeans I had met in Paris. Young displaced persons were common enough in those days. In many ways they were much the same as the other foreign students. They were different in that they seemed to be involved in a great burning love affair with their countries, whereas the others were not. To an American their homesickness was often hard to understand. Not that I did not love America or New York or the abstract idea of my native land. I did. Yet it was on another level than that of the Poles, the Czechs, the Hungarians, the Serbs I knew. My feelings had little in common with theirs. I could understand that difference, of course, but my sympathy with it was occasionally jarred by a cold voice inside me which rejected as dangerous or spurious or sometimes both their exaggerated nationalism.

Mihailo's nostalgia was different. He did not seem to yearn for one small Slavic corner but rather for them all. He never put his own rootlessness in terms of his individual loss but rather as a part of the loss of millions of people displaced, deported, uprooted, exiled all over this curious post-war map of Europe. Not that he saw himself as universal, no. Yet he could not place his own personal experience in any other context than that of one out of millions of others.

What words did he use to convey this to me? How did he say this in his funny, correct, bookish English? I do not remember now. I remember only a feeling of understanding for him, a sense of admiration for his simplicity, his honesty, his lack of rancour. He was so far removed from my left-wing

47

intellectual friends, from my whole world of liberal-cum-progressive father, background, upbringing, including the prevailing note of 1948 among university students in general. He was so far removed from everything I had ever known yet he was so easy to recognise, to meet, to understand, to love.

The canals. Those strange *quais*, great blocks of ugly houses yet trees and a light totally different from others in this city of singular lights and shadows. Canal de l'Ourcq. Flanders, the Baltic, the North. And the slow barges with Belgian or Dutch flags and small pots of ivy or geraniums growing near the wheel inside, clothes flapping on lines above loads of gravel or sand.

The wind played with our faces.

"Cold?" he asked.

"A little."

"Look!" he pointed, laughing. There on the corner, facing the lock, was a tiny grey café-hotel crazily named "Café du Midi". In this northern, this Frisian state.

We went in, flushed from the wind. The owner was behind the bar. He looked at us with curiosity and waved us to a table near the window, and near the stove. It was a very ordinary little café but even then, in those first minutes, I was aware of a certain uncommon warmth. From the window we could see the locks, the amazing mechanism of the water levels, the green, tree-lined alleys, the autumn russet of the leaves.

"I'm going to come back here and sketch one day," I said, cupping my hands over a glass of *vin chaud*. Mihailo got up and went over to the patron. In a minute he was back with a pad and three pencils.

"Now," he said. "Not 'one day'. Now."

I sketched him first, but badly, and threw it away impatiently. Then the scrap of view from the window, then the patron who had joined us at the table, filling our glasses with Beaujolais "to loosen up my fingers", he said. We laughed continuously, the three of us.

The patron was from Toulon. His café there had been bombed out during the war so he came to Paris. His wife was Parisienne, he explained. She took advantage of the catastrophes of war to get him to give up the sun of the Midi and live in this "bronchitis trap", he said. The canal outside was as much as Paris offered in the way of a port, he told us, so he bought the café and baptised it "du Midi". Monsieur Jean's southern accent and his Mediterranean gestures were enough to warm any conversation, however cold the weather outside.

He took the sketches I left on the table and with charming ceremony hung them over the bar with thumb tacks. "Who knows, who knows," he said, "if the café owner in Arles had been more farsighted about Van Gogh's pictures . . . I'm not taking any chances." He cocked his head to one side and looked at his portrait. "Besides, she flatters me."

He came back to the table and poured another glass of wine. "Bon. Since I have suddenly become a patron of the arts and since I haven't laughed like this for ages, let me invite you to a bouillabaisse dinner. Come back about eight. I'll show you what a real bouillabaisse is. Not this slop they serve you in Paris. A real one. And you will meet my wife."

Out on the street we couldn't quite believe it.

"Do you think he meant it?" asked Mihailo, incredulous.

"Of course, he wouldn't have said it otherwise," I replied. People have always been warm to me. Mihailo remained incredulous.

"Do you know that I have been in Paris for two years and I have still to be invited to a French home? And in one afternoon with you it happens . . . just like that," he said, snapping his fingers. "You are amazing," and he laughed out loud. "I feel that something very wonderful has happened to me."

"It has," and I laughed too.

We followed the canals, watching the day close in around us. We walked along the Canal de l'Ourcq for hours, talking, laughing, sometimes running to get warm, sometimes sitting on green embankments waving to barge keepers or to their children who played land games like jacks or jump-rope on slippery decks, red-cheeked children who smiled or waved back at us on the cobblestones of the quais.

A long table was set at the back of the café. There was a white tablecloth and a bowl of flowers in the centre. Madame Nicole, the patron's wife, was a faded little woman in her fifties, as quiet as Jean was volatile. She looked on his enthusiasm with pleasure, welcoming us because Jean had welcomed us.

Mihailo had never eaten *bouillabaisse*. As he took off his raincoat I noticed Jean looking at him, his big frame so very thin.

"So," he said, "this is a Russian," savouring the idea. "And you are American. Odd mixture these days. One sees everything in Paris, eh, ma petite Nicole? But in Toulon there were funny mixtures, too. Do you remember the English milady who married her Martiniquais sailor? Lady whatwashername. Big black fellow. He sat on her yacht afterwards giving orders to the others. Before the war. Ah, oui. Toulon had its day, too. Full of horrible new buildings now. Ugh."

They served Mihailo huge helpings of fish and broth and garlic bread. And the *rouille*! That miraculous sauce! Jean was very proud of his *rouille* and was overjoyed at my appreciation. I had eaten several good *bouillabaisses* in the Midi and told him, without exaggerating, that his was the best I had tasted. And the *rouille* was incomparable. But it was

Mihailo that he concentrated on feeding. The wine, the giddy meridional conversation, the tall tales Jean told made us all slightly drunk. The more Jean drank the thicker his accent became and the funnier were his stories as a result.

It was close to twelve when we began to leave. Mihailo explained to them that he had to be in at twelve. Jean could not get over Mihailo's being a theology student. "I knew he was something special, as soon as I saw him I knew that. But a Russian priest. Well," he added doubtfully.

Nicole pointed out that that was pretty special after all. Mihailo laughed good-naturedly. We left amid much hand-shaking and many promises to come back soon and often.

Mihailo and I walked slowly. I found it hard to believe that twelve hours ago the boy at my side was someone who had not come to lunch last week, an irritant, a haunting irritant. And now after this long enchanting day I felt an indescribable bond with him.

"Here, I will take you to the métro." We walked along quietly, still smiling.

At the métro entrance, cold now and windy, he took my hand. "Tomorrow," he began hesitantly. "Could you . . . could we go for another walk tomorrow?" The wind blew around us.

"Thirty, rue du Dragon. Twelve noon. And this time I won't come looking . . ."

He laughed. "Chez Madame Ferson. Twelve noon. Fourth floor. Goodnight, Christmas Carol. And merci."

That was the beginning, the timid beginning. And the end is now in a hotel room on the Boulevard Raspail fifteen years later.

I had walked slowly down the Boulevard Raspail to my hotel, seeing him, seeing him smile, laugh, seeing him walk next to me, seeing him in my room on the rue du Dragon, hearing his voice, listening to him talking quietly or watching him as he listened to me or to music or to others. How could he have walked away, how could he have left me? Alexis? Was it Alexis who made him do it? But how could he have been brought to it? Where is he now, Mihailo? Oh Christ, where is he now?

Chapter Eight

I COULD hear the bells of Saint-Germain-des-Prés striking twelve when he knocked on the door. He came that day, hich was the second Sunday in November, entering the room timidly, still unsure.

"It is a nice room, isn't it?" he said, looking around at the bright curtains and the red cabbage roses of the bedspread.

"I use the armoire as a guest room," I laughed. "Did you ever see anything so enormous?"

We had lunch at a table by the window, looking out over the rooftops.

"I've forgotten what it is like, to live in a nice room," he said with a funny smile. "We are twenty in a dormitory now."

"Twenty!"

"It shocks you?"

"Well, perhaps not shock. But it can't be very pleasant, I mean ... unless you are all the same age or something ..."

"No. You are right. It is not very pleasant. And we are not all the same age. There are several old men ..."

"Old men? Studying theology?"

"Yes. There is no age limit ..."

I could see that it had pained him to have to tell me, an outsider, that his seminary was not all it should have been. Effortlessly, we talked of other things, listened to music, looked at sketches or at pictures I had taken over the summer. We went for a walk that afternoon and on into the evening. And in the days that followed we saw each other as often as possible.

53

In the very beginning we avoided Claude and my friends, almost unconsciously. I sensed that Mihailo felt somewhat uncomfortable with them. Besides, there was so much to do, to see during the hours that we were together that I did not really want anyone else with us. Yet the main reason was not that. But it took time before I really understood it myself. It was not because Mihailo was a theological student, not because of the fundamental difference in their characters, but simply a question of money.

Student scholarships varied in 1948. I suppose they do still. For instance, a Spanish painter friend of mine was getting ten thousand francs a month, which was terribly low. American GIs were getting seventy-five dollars a month, or thirty-five thousand francs a month, plus a yearly allotment for books, tuition, and inscription or lab fees. Tor was sending me the same amount—but he also sent me presents of money for Christmas, vacations, extra clothing, or just tucked a ten-dollar bill into a letter "for stamps", as he put it. Claude's mother gave him fifty thousand francs a month plus an apartment; he was enormously well off for a student and managed to feed half of Saint-Germain-des-Prés. But Mihailo had three thousand francs a month. That was the equivalent of six or seven dollars. He had a free room—that is, a bed in a dormitory. But the three thousand francs were supposed to do for everything else, including food.

Mihailo was hungry. Not the kind of hunger that you can appease with one good meal, but hungry to the point where hunger had become an obsession. To eat enough, to have enough to eat was peace, an aim, a heaven of a kind. Several weeks before we met he had fallen on a crazy job, translating a long Russian text into English. He was given ten thousand francs, which was ridiculously underpaid. But the notion, the vision of ten thousand francs was so enormous, so incredible to him that he trembled with fear at the thought of not getting the job. When I met Mihailo he had eaten enough, or reasonably enough, for nearly a fortnight. The pervasive pains of hunger had ceased to follow him through the days and nights. He still had some money left to ration his meals out over a period of another fortnight. The one luxury he had permitted himself, the one glimpse of something from a realm other than that of strict survival, was to see Open City.

I had read of hunger. Just recently I had read Orwell on hunger, but I had never been confronted with anyone who had suffered it, who was diseased with it as was Mihailo. His big body, over six feet tall, gaunt, his frame which should have been heavy, was thin and vulnerable. I cooked lunch that Sunday and dinner and would have cooked lunch, dinner and breakfast all week long with high teas in between but he had to "learn his catechism". He was only free on Wednesday nights and weekends then.

Those early weeks, through November and December, went by noiselessly, marked by the timidity of awakening love.

Once we went to the theatre. We saw *Occupe-toi d'Amélie* at the Marigny with Jean-Louis Barrault and Madeleine Renault. Claude came with us and took us to Les Halles for onion soup afterwards. Another time we went to a Segovia concert. Mihailo was thrilled; he loved Segovia, though I didn't know it, and he knew a good deal about Spanish music. How he had ever crowded such things as a love for de Falla into a life seemingly blocked out by war, prison camps, starvation and seminaries, amazed me.

During those weeks, as we grew to know each other, as he relaxed, as he unbent and became more sure of himself, less withdrawn, I realised that I had found in Mihailo a kind of love, an odd kind of love quite apart from anything I had ever imagined love could be. An enormous tenderness, an engulfing tenderness, as though my affection for this tall, gaunt boy was a fragile gift given to me, mysteriously, quietly, from very far away.

"I will miss you over the holidays. I wish you would come. Claude's mother wouldn't mind at all, you know."

"And how I wish I could go. But my cousin is coming from Heidelberg to be with me. I could not disappoint him."

"No, I suppose not. But it seems silly to give up a chance to relax in the sun . . ."

I left for Cannes somewhat less lightheartedly than I had anticipated. Before leaving, I dropped off a package of canned meats and butter with Jean at the Café du Midi, asking him to get it to Mihailo in time for Christmas. I couldn't go to Cannes leaving him with his soup-kitchen meals and three thousand francs.

Late at night, huddled in a corner of the under-heated train, I saw with clarity that I was deeply in love. Irrevocably in love. A confusing patchwork of images filled my mind, conundrums without answers . . . an Orthodox priest?

Chapter Nine

CANNES was an electric blue that Christmas. The sun was bright and warm, the hillsides still green, that matt Mediterranean green of laurel and rosemary and pines. Claude was at the station to meet me, looking sleepy and sun-tanned. Mimosa and orange trees, palms and dates, grape-vines and jasmine. After grey, foggy Paris it takes time to believe in the Côte d'Azur.

Big fires blazed in the downstairs rooms. Claude had brought along Philippe and an American photographer, Alan Karr. Monique and Fred were pleased to see me looking well and immediately recruited me into the feverish kitchen, where a completely Anglo-Saxon Christmas was in preparation. Turkey, pumpkin pies, mince pies, Christmas pudding, cranberry sauce, chestnuts, what else? They did not go along with candied sweet potatoes but Alan and I imposed American vetoes on Christmas without them. On Christmas day we were sixteen at table, a huge Spanish table set with an eccentric assortment of crockery and glasses.

Karr looked at it after he had helped set the table and laughed, "It looks as if the food editor at *House and Garden* had run amok."

Christmas trees abounded. I did one in the garden, Claude decorated the living-room one, Fred made a wooden one on the terrace which was the best of all. And under the bright Christmas sun we played tennis or wandered around the port of Cannes in sweaters. We played *boules* at the Casino and won. We lost it at roulette. I had never been in a casino before,

57

found it hard to concentrate on the game, was constantly distracted by the intensity of the real gamblers.

A party for New Year's Eve? Why? Every day was a party. No need to make it special. Champagne *en plus*, that was all. There were about twenty people, most of them neighbours. Someone played the piano and we danced. Someone else brought over a record collection. We finished the champagne and drank Fred's own rosé.

I looked round the room at Monique, at Fred and at Claude and thought of my father. How like him they were. There was never any real dissension in this house, nor had there been in Tor's. No unhappiness that was not counteracted by their own innate gift for happiness. I felt an overwhelming gratitude for the love, the warmth that they, like Tor, had given me. The happy few.

Two more days and back to Paris. I was to return alone. Claude and Philippe were going to spend a few days in Geneva with Philippe's family. I wrote to Mihailo, asking him to meet me at the Gare de Lyon. The last of the sunshine, the mimosa and the orange trees, through the night train's joggling back to Paris.

And there he was, pale, tall, thin, that incomparable smile which generated a light of its own on the smoky platform.

"Salut."

"Salut."

"You are beautiful. So brown. Was it sunny all the time in Cannes?"

"Fantastic. We took sunbaths on the terrace. On New Year's Day we went sailing. You should have come. On Christmas day there were sixteen at table. Claude's mother is an angel."

"Yes, I see. You are a lovely colour. Here it has rained. No sun."

"Come on. Let's go to the Dragon flat. La Ferson is still away, I think. We can make lots of noise."

"Claude is not with you?"

"No. He stayed on. I came back a few days earlier."

"Oh, why? You should have stayed and enjoyed the sun. Look how dreary Paris is . . ." And I looked up at him, straight at him, his clear brown eyes looking at mine.

"No. It's not dreary at all." We stood looking at each other. He finally lowered his eyes and took my suitcase.

Once at the flat I begged for time to take a bath before fixing lunch. "Let me fix lunch while you bathe," Mihailo offered.

"No, don't bother. I've got it all in my suitcase. Go and read a book or something. I'll only be a minute."

When I came out I found him on the bed fast asleep, his face turned to the wall. I walked over to him, softly, not to wake him, and I looked down at his face in repose, the chin no longer stubborn, the mouth not tense but like a child's at peace, his dark hair ruffled on the pillow, the beautiful lines of his cheek-bones rather like a girl's, so fine. Yet there was nothing feminine about him. His height, his broad frame, thin perhaps but strong, despite his thinness still strong.

I watched him sleep, wondering what I should be feeling. Something, surely. Because I had decided in that minute that Mihailo should make love to me; I decided it then and there, looking at him asleep. I put aside any idea that he wouldn't want to, that being a theological student might prevent him. When a twenty-year-old girl decides that this is it, the decision, so immensely important in itself, cannot be rendered complicated by Orthodox dogma. It was my monemt, not Byzantium's.

I was still looking at him, but lost in my dialogue with the Russian saints I failed to notice that Mihailo was awake, smiling at me.

"You look angry," he said, propping himself up on one elbow. "Is it because I fell asleep?"

"No. I . . . I was trying not to wake you," and I sat down on the edge of the bed, no saints in my mind now.

He was rubbing his shoulder.

"Shall I give you a massage? I'm great at massages!" I climbed across the bed, kneeling over him. He took my hand. I started to massage his shoulder when I saw his face close to mine.

"Don't, Carola, don't . . ." Then I was in his arms, kissing him harder and harder, holding him close to me, wild and frantic, my hands rushing past his shirt to his smooth skin, his smooth, broad back.

"You don't know what you are doing. . . ." his voice hoarse close to my ear, his shirt undone.

"I love you, Mihailo. I love you. It's all right. I love you."

"But you have never . . ."

"No. Never. But I want you . . . you."

"Carola . . ."

"Don't say anything. If I love you it's all right . . . and in a way, in a small way, you must love me, a little."

He looked at me, brushing back my hair with his hand, smiling. "A little, oh yes, a little," and then kissing me closer and closer, panic and fire, heat and love in great waves convulsing me, bringing me to Mihailo.

"Sh. Don't talk. Give me your hand to hold."

It is not necessarily easy to become lovers, not for everyone. We were awkward, shy, avoided each other's nakedness, groping through the shells of our childhoods to a world of adult emotions, yet clothing those emotions in the innocence we knew. This slow awakening of our bodies was as tender, as frank as the awakening of our friendship, our love for each other. We knew nothing of the physical love that went on unconcernedly around us. Our love was different, younger, eternal, free of fear, of stress. And we both knew it. We seemed to dream through the winter, that timeless winter fifteen years ago.

Chapter Ten

ONE freezing afternoon we were chatting with Jean at the Café du Midi. The bistro was warm, a huge Godin coal stove blazed in the middle of the room.

Jean, behind the bar, interrupted a story he was telling, looked up at me and said impulsively, "Why don't you rent my top room!" Not a question but an exclamation. "It has a big window . . . you can see way up and down the canal. Come on. Come and see."

He darted out from behind the bar, agile in his roundness, and we followed him, exchanging glances of surprise. Jean kept talking as we walked up the short flights of stairs. I had never been in a hotel proper. The corridors, small and bright, were lighted by large windows. The wallpaper was of faded roses, the kind one tends to associate with obscure French hotels. On the third floor, Jean, alternately talking and puffing from the fast climb up, pushed open the door to a large room, bright even in that February half-light. It had not been used for years, Jean explained, but with a coat of paint and some furniture. . .

"Look at that view!" He stood at the window, rubbing the panes so that we could see better.

I looked at Mihailo questioningly. "You could paint here . . ." he said, his eyes showing the excitement his voice concealed.

Jean, that most perceptive of men, said in a booming voice, "Agreed. It's done," and proceeded to set a price which was ridiculously low and a date on which I could move in, which was almost immediately. Before we had a chance even to thank him he was out of the room and on his way down the stairs, the two of us following him in gales of laughter.

"We have a house! Our own house!" The amazing luck of it all! "I sometimes think you must be a witch," Mihailo said, shaking his head.

On Saturday we started off early to the Flea Market. The day before Jean had someone in to wash down the room. After the Flea Market expedition we spent the rest of the day painting it.

What wonderful junk we picked up. A huge painting of a shepherdess in a sylvan setting, complete with gigantic gold plaster frame. I painted a goatee and moustache on the shepherdess and added a satyr sticking his head out from under a strategic bush, and I signed it Dali. We picked up a veteran Algerian pouf which we stuffed full of old rags and newspapers, so one could sit on it. And whenever one did, it squeaked terribly. We bought a huge mirror which made you look wobbly and long, and we hung it outside the door, "to encourage visitors", we laughed. Then the rug. A beautiful old rug with a hole in it the size of an armchair. We put the pouf in the middle of the hole and found it looked like a dart board seen from above. We painted the room white and hung blue and white striped curtains on the big window overlooking the canal. A few watercolours on the walls, sketches tacked up, along with reproductions here and there, the big bed Jean provided, the inevitable French wardrobe, a screen around the sink in the corner and, near the window, my easel with a half-finished portrait of Mihailo.

That was it. Each object, each corner was a point of affection, each shadow and light a familiar warmth, linking us together. I have started other homes since, happy homes with the noise of four children, but never have I equalled the warmth of the top-floor room overlooking the Canal de l'Ourcq.

On Wednesdays Mihailo was free from four o'clock until noon on Thursdays. I took to meeting him at the little café on the rue Meynardier, and we walked along the canals if the weather was half-way good. We often ate with Jean and Nicole, both of whom tried hard to stuff Mihailo full of meat and eggs and butter, eyeing him surreptitiously for signs of putting on weight. One evening Nicole confided to me that Jean had had TB as a young man, through malnutrition, overwork, and "lack of love", as he put it. He seemed to sniff the symptoms in Mihailo. Occasionally, I would catch him looking at Mihailo with an odd expression in his eyes, a sadness with a touch of anger. Then, with an abrupt gesture, he would move down the bar and serve a customer or wipe an already clean glass, muttering to himself. Though he never put it into words, I understood mutely that his gesture, his half-heard curses, were directed to whatever powers there were that permit boys like Mihailo to go through life as "emmerdé" as he so obviously was.

Claude was waiting for me at the Grande Chaumière the next Monday. I had not told him about the room, nor about the Hotel du Midi. Not yet. But I saw Claude almost as much as before. Except on Wednesdays. On weekends, up until we took the room, we sometimes joined Claude and the others at a party or at the Flore. There was a difference between before the Christmas holidays and after, a difference which none of us spoke of but of which we were all aware, each in his own way.

"Hello. I've been waiting for you for hours. Why are these painting people always so late!" he grinned. "Look, there's a new club opening Wednesday night. Camus is going to be there, all the Rose Rouge types, Greco, everyone. Want to come?" Before I could refuse, he added in a sweeter tone than I had ever heard him use, "Bring Mihailo, he'd probably like it."

64

"Oh. . . ." I was suddenly embarrassed, though not sure why. We were silent for a moment. I felt him looking at me. He was smiling gently when I finally brought my eyes up to meet his.

"Happy?"

I nodded my head.

"Well, that's what we wanted, wasn't it?"

We both grinned, but just a tiny bit wistfully, I thought.

"We'll meet at the Tabou about ten thirty, unless you want to have dinner at the flat earlier?" I nodded.

"Oh, by the way. I've been accepted at RADA for next year," he added.

Casually, so very casually.

"Claude! That's wonderful. I mean, for you it's wonderful. But that means you'll have to live in London." It suddenly struck me that Paris was unthinkable without Claude.

"Eh, oui, ma cocotte. You can send me CARE packages with vin ordinaire and Camemberts."

We walked along the Boulevard Montparnasse, noisy with late afternoon traffic. "It will be like the end of something, you know. Paris without you. I'm not sure I like the idea at all."

"Well, let's not weep till September. That's a long time off . . ."

Mihailo had never been to a night club. He had never heard of the Tabou or the Rose Rouge, but he knew Camus by heart. The Tabou was crowded at ten-thirty. We squeezed up the bar, past a pair of Negro jazz musicians Claude knew, and the three of us waited for the others to arrive. As I said hello to people Mihailo looked about, amused at the beautiful girls in exaggerated clothes. There was a devastating blonde, tall and handsome, who wore a flame-coloured fullskirt down past her calves, a gold corset-like belt, and a black jersey top cut deep between her breasts. She must have been six feet tall.

Some kind of North African earrings hung down nearly to her shoulders. She jangled slightly as she walked.

Mihailo grinned at me as she inched by. He was enjoying himself. I was so relieved. Just before going down the steps, I had felt a pang of fear; suppose he hates the place, suppose he objects to bars like this, suppose we have a quarrel? The notion of a row with Mihailo filled me with terror. I could not imagine getting angry with him, and was ill at the thought that he could get angry with me. Especially over the Tabou. But there was no fight. Not then nor ever.

Philippe finally showed up, and with him an odd assortment of "copains", the dreadful Pretzel included. She looked at Mihailo, gave a gorgeous little stage titter, and leapt over to him.

"Oh, that lovely boy again, you're back!" Claude pulled her away before she climbed up Mihailo's chest. "Let go, imbecile, I've loved him ever since the night we ate the frites, real love, moi, je le sais. . . . "

Poor Pretzel. She ended up marrying an ex-GI and settled in Topeka, Kansas, where she must have the oddest memories in town.

Mihailo was amused by the Tabou, amused by the new night club which was off the Champs Elysées, and rather impressed by the presence of Greco, Camus, Prévert, Adamov and a cross-section of Saint-Germain-des-Prés citizenry whose names were catch-words in the domain of films, theatre or the plastic arts. The owner of the club was a remarkably beautiful Martiniquaise singer who seemed to know everyone on both sides of the Atlantic. She was a friend of Tor's, too.

We were dancing together for the first time.

"I'm amazed that you ever had the time to learn how to dance, what with wars and camps and bishops and all." He smiled, holding me very close.

"I thought I would be the only one here in a sweater and

no jacket. I was almost going to refuse to come. But look over there, there is someone else without a jacket, and there, too."

"I told you so."

"Ah, but I did not believe you. I thought you were just being nice."

"No. It's that sort of place. A lot of people dress like you on purpose. It's a kind of affectation."

"Hah! And I would give anything to have just one white shirt and just one suit . . . a real suit. Like other people have. If I ever have any money I am going to change shirts three times a day. For each meal . . ."

"You'll never have any money. You'll spend it all on food," I laughed.

"Oh, who knows. I might make money. In business. Or something."

I looked up at him, surprised.

"Can Orthodox priests be businessmen, too?"

He pulled me to him, hesitated before answering.

"No. Not Orthodox priests."

"Well, then?"

"I am not a priest yet . . ."

I caught my breath. So many things crystallised in my mind, in that tiny moment, so many half-hopes, unformed wishes that I had never allowed to take shape, all seemed to fit together like the pieces in a puzzle, in that tiny moment. I do not know what instinct told me not to pursue the question any further, Later on, later on.

That night, holding him to me, following the lines of his face, his cheeks, his brow, with my fingers, I realised that my life would be half a life without Mihailo.

Fifteen years later on the Boulevard Raspail I know still that I was right.

Chapter Eleven

THE clamour of the telephone made me jump. Why should the telephone ring for me in the Hotel Cayré? Perhaps the children . . .

"A call from London, Madame."

"Thank you."

"Carola. Are you there, Carola! Can you hear me?"

"Claude?" My voice incredulous. No, not Claude, not now.

"Yes. Look. I'm just taking off for London airport. I'll be at Le Bourget in under two hours. Can you meet me?"

Le Bourget in two hours.

"What?" I asked groggily.

"Carola. Please. Are you all right?" His voice was patient and impatient at once.

"Yes. I'm fine."

"Did you. . . Have you seen anyone?"

"No." I heard his breath relax.

"Well, then."

"Claude. What is all this? Why should you come galloping over here . . ."

"Never mind that now. I love galloping. Remember, the airport in less than two hours."

"But why? Why should you come here?" I felt my hands grow cold, my scalp tightening with fear. My voice seemed to fail me.

"Please, Carola. I can't explain now. They are calling my

68

flight. Please do this for me. In the way I ask done." His voice was taut, unlike him.

"All right. I will."

I looked at my watch. Six forty. How early it was. Of course. It must be early still.

I changed into a warm turtle-necked wool dress and washed my face. In the big old-fashioned bathroom I combed my hair automatically. It seemed redundant, somehow. A raincoat, a purse with cigarettes, lighter and French francs, the heavy hotel room key in my hand. And once again the Boulevard Raspail.

Panic welled up within me, then receded like waves in an uncertain sea. Then Claude has known something all along. But known what? That Mihailo is married to some nice French girl and lives in the suburbs? that he never loved me? that it was all a figment of my imagination? that I went through madness and despair for nothing, a dream? that Mihailo is now balding and prosperous with drawers full of shirts... is that what Claude knows? What else could he know that he would have had to hide from me? What else? Why should he take a plane like this in the middle of the evening to tell me Mihailo is here in Paris? I know he is here. I have always known it. What then? To tell me Mihailo would be embarrassed by me now? I know that, too. I won't look for him. Not now. Only the Select and there is no one left in the Select. Doesn't he know that there is no one left anywhere? That I am not left either? That Claude himself is not left? Does he have to take a plane crazily without notice on this exhausting day to tell me everything I know? And to see for himself that I still love that boy. That all these years have fallen at my feet like nothing ... that children and Gavin are nothing at all compared to that boy ... thathe has lived within me since then and that no matter what Claude will find to tell me now, Mihailo will continue as he always has, since

69

I first set eyes on him fifteen years ago. The waves of panic subsided and I grew calmer, numbed by my own weariness.

Once on the street I was suddenly devoured by curiosity. I walked down the rue de Rennes to the Flore, my footsteps quick and impatient. On the Boulevard Saint-Germain there were knots of people between the Deux Magots and the Flore. The rue Saint-Benoit was like the main street of a small town, crowded with people going nowhere, just standing. I looked at the faces around the terrace tables, looked at them carefully as though I were seeking out someone, then inside the café, carefully again, each table, the waiters, the mirrors, and upstairs, too. I came out of the Flore and walked toward the river. There was time yet.

The kids at the Flore, the young ones, were all clean and neat, well dressed. In this spring they wore well-cut blazers, clean shirts, good shirts, expensive sweaters, nicely pressed trousers, Burberrys. The girls, too—boutique clothes, cashmere sweaters, Esterel capes, Courreges boots.

Another generation, no war at their heels. Only one or two of the waiters remained. 1948 seems a very long time ago here.

Claude. I am being unfair to Claude. The only link with that childhood, that faraway world of 1948. A well-known London actor now, he lives again one street away just as he did then, when I lived on the rue du Dragon and he on the rue des Saints-Pères.

We never discuss Mihailo, not for years, not since I came back to Europe married to Gavin, with two of my children still in diapers.

There was once, when my youngest son was born, an exchange of looks, an awkward moment. My sister-in-law asked what we were going to call the baby. As usual, we didn't have a name.

She said, "Why not Michael?"

Claude's eyes flashed at me. I could feel myself colouring. Gavin, who resolutely refuses to hold with what he terms "this mystique", but Gavin who is infinitely kind, got up and began making drinks and offering other suggestions in honour of a variety of Welsh uncles. When he came over to me with a drink in his hand, he looked down very gently, tenderness and understanding in his eyes for which I was immensely grateful.

In 1955 Claude met us at Southampton and drove us up to London. It was so marvellous to see him, unchanged, utterly unchanged, the crazy humour, flights of word fantasy, inane jokes, the most exhilarating man I have ever known.

Late that night, the children in bed, Gavin on the telephone to his mother in Wales, we looked at each other with no jokes, no laughter in our eyes.

"I tried to find him, you know. Those bearded bastards at that flea trap wouldn't help. They were rude, said ugly things about him, about you. Only Alexis, that sweet relation, remained. I found him by sitting alternately at the Coupole and the Select until he turned up. I had only seen him once and wasn't sure it was he. But it was. The waiter at the Select told me it was. He was polite, but only just. Mihailo was away, he said. He didn't know where. If you wanted to write him you might try writing him at Alexis's address and if he heard from Mihailo he'd forward it. I asked the address and he said, he bloody well sneered, care of the Select, Boulevard Montparnasse, Paris 14.

"I'm ashamed to say I did not punch his face in. We sat down and I tried to reason with him. But he maintained his position, arrogant—enjoying it. You know. Like a little boy pulling off a fly's wings. Then he finally said, as a sort of dismissal, 'It would never occur to Carola, of course, to think that Mihailo might have had enough?' I must say that floored me. The bastard."

We were silent for some time, "You know," I finally said, "even that doesn't make sense. He would have written. Even it that were true he would have written. It just doesn't make sense. I left him Tor's address, the name of the school, everything. He wasn't well when I left Paris, that cough and a cold he couldn't shake . . . The Hotel du Midi had already closed, remember? We were staying in a room on Monsieur le Prince. But it was only temporary. He hadn't been back to the seminary in months but he had arranged with a friend to have his mail sent there. Serge, the boy's name was. I don't think you knew him. Serge. Mihailo's parents wrote him there, too, care of Serge. He told me to use that address because he didn't know what hotel he would move to. You were in London then. Oh Christ! If you hadn't been in London he would have seen you, I'm sure. I know it was Alexis who did this. But how? What could have made him listen? What could anyone have said to make him stop loving me? He knew! And he was stubborn . . . Claude, remember him? He was stubborn, you couldn't change his mind easily. He knew I loved him . . . He knew, he knew . . ." And I was crying.

Out of the silence, Claude's voice, his low, incredulous voice reached me. "You still love him."

I did not answer. I did not have to.

That was in 1955. We never spoke of him again. In another way I love Gavin. I have an extremely busy life, I have four children. We never spoke of him again, that's all.

Walking toward the river in the rue Bonaparte a wave of cold fear paralysed me. What does Claude know? Why is he flying here to tell me something he could have told me yesterday or any day for the past eight years in London? Tears blur the outline of the street. And in my mind's eye the persistent circle of light revolves around the question, round and round, light and fire in darkness. Who did this to me, who severed me, who slashed me in two? Where is Alexis now? Who did this, who, if not I?

Chapter Twelve

"You know," he mused, "we have two worlds together, you and I. It is as though we wore Mardi Gras masks— put them on, take them off, two different sets of us."

We were sitting on the edge of the quai at the tip of the Ile de la Cité, the prow-like tip under the statue of Henri IV. It was the first warm day, in March.

"When we are here on the Left Bank, with the others, with Claude and Philippe and all the others, we are one kind of us. And when we are alone at the hotel, near the canals, along the canals, we are another us. It is not the same us that sits in cafés here, not the same that walks by the locks."

He twisted around on his stomach, to see my reaction. I did not say anything. He continued. "The other us is private. More...more real. Or less real, maybe. Yes. Probably less real."

"I'm real," I answered quietly.

He was looking down at the grass, the blades of thin city grass growing around the cobblestones. His fingers brushed over the grass lightly, back and forth, as one might brush over feathers, just to see what they feel like.

"I am not sure you are real," he said slowly. "I am not sure that you are here, that this is your hand, that this is your shoulder, that it is your breath making the grass move slightly. I am not at all sure."

He turned over again, impatiently, sat with his arms around his knees. I could no longer see his face.

"Do you know how people lost in the desert see mirages? Do you know what hallucinations are? Hunger can create hallucinations of a kind. Not only hunger for food, but

74

hunger for . . . for affection, for some sort of . . . of love, for someone who looks at you knowing you are there, someone who is warm when everything else is cold. Someone who . . . who is . . . a hallucination, a mirage when you are alone. Once in a while I wake up—oh, even when I am not asleep—but I wake up and I am cold and afraid because I suddenly know that you are a mirage, that I am hungry again, that I am going to scream because there is no you. There is only an emptiness, the emptiness I know so well, all over my body."

Moved, my throat tight, I reached out for him, touched him with my hand.

"I'm real. You don't have to be afraid." He was silent, his head averted.

"Mihailo?"

But he did not answer. He sat there mutely looking at the grass.

Today, fifteen years later on a mild spring evening I see other young couples strolling along the tip of the Île de la Cité, sitting on the grass in the still warm sun. But the big oak at the foot of the staircase, the beautiful big oak is no longer there. It was cut down as the result of a bad storm. Changeless Paris, unchanged Paris, eternal Paris. Except in small details.

Then the fine spring rain made patterns on the window, drawing designs of cubes and arrows, lace and castles among the fragments of trees, leaves and shadows outside. I had been working on the portrait all Saturday afternoon. It was a difficult portrait. I found it hard to see him, to understand the light, to feel the eyes. Mihailo came into the room about five o'clock. How many months had it been? Yet each time he appeared I felt that curious surge of joy and pleasure in seeing him smile in welcome.

"Going well?" he asked, looking at the easel. "Ouf. Do I look as sad as all that?" and he made a face at the painting. "The melancholic Slav?".

"Or just a priest?" I grinned back at him.

I kept on working, not paying much attention to him. From time to time I was aware of his steps, noticed vaguely that he was either at the window or sitting on the bed reading. But I was not really paying much attention. Eventually, however, I glanced over at him and was arrested by his expression, looking at me darkly, almost coldly from his seat on the bed.

"What's the matter?"

He got up and took a cigarette.

"Matter. English is a strange language. Matter, materialism, What's the matter? Where is the matter? Matter, spirit, salvation, abnegation, love, God, peace, the flesh, war, blood, hunger, youth, the Holy Ghost. . . . "

"What's all this?" I said, horrified. Yet intuitively I knew that this would happen sooner or later. "What's all this?"

"Nothing. I'm sorry."

"Come on. Out with it."

"There is nothing to be out with . . . "

"You mean you don't want to hurt me."

"No. I do not want to hurt you. But I don't mean that. It's . . . it's not you . . . it's me."

"You mean the sins of the flesh and all that."

"And all that. As you say. Do you know what all that is? No. Of course you do not. Do you know that we are committing a mortal sin? Do you know that we are defiling a sacrament? Do you know that I am defiling a sacrament?"

"I do not! I certainly do not!" I answered heatedly. "And any dogma that says you are is bloody well off its . . . "

"Why? Because love or need or affection is all-powerful, excuses its own excesses, justifies everything? No. That is not true. Or that biological explanations with Freudian terms explain away the Commandments? They do not."

"Mihailo. What has happened to you?"

"Nothing has happened. That is, everything has happened but I have refused to face it. Because I cannot afford to lose you. I cannot afford to say—well, I've given in to sins of the flesh but it was all a mistake and anyway I am young and I like making love but I am too poor to marry and she is a very forward girl, very American, very modern, therefore I fell, but it was all a mistake and I won't do it again. No. I cannot say that. I am not a hypocrite, after all. And you are not all that forward, for that matter..."

"Go on," I urged. "Talk about it. Are you 'living in sin' according to ... to your standards?"

"And according to yours, too, I hope."

"No. Not according to mine. Not at all."

"But you are not amoral, surely!"

"No. I don't think so. I love you, that's all. Not to live with you would be unnatural and hypocritical and I would not be any more honest to myself for it ..."

"For 'it'? For depriving yourself of a pleasure to which you have no right, you mean?"

"But I do have the right! My body is my own, governed by a perfectly sound mind. I am not abusing my body. I'm doing with it what it was created to do ... honestly. I love you..."

"Therefore I have you," he interrupted.

"And that's amoral or immoral?" I asked.

"Yes, of course it is."

I was silent.

"Carola, don't you see how false I am being?"

"No!" But in a way I did. I had never been able to face the question of Mihailo's vocation, his status as a seminarian, his future as a priest. In a sense it embarrassed me. I felt acute

77

discomfort at the thought of being in love with an Orthodox priest. I had never known an Orthodox Christian, let alone a clergyman, in my life . . . I had no idea of what or how they believed, how they felt about sex or anything else for that matter. All I did know about them was that their seminarians were half-starved and had no winter coats or shoes. That, I supposed, was not a matter of dogma, however.

"Yes, yes, winter coats and no money and hypocrisy. Yes. I know, I know, I know. But every time I come into this room, every time I reach out to find you and finding you hold you, everytime I love you I go through a moment of near drowning . . ."

"Good heavens, Mihailo! Don't you have any doubts about what you've been taught? Do you honestly believe you are doing wrong, that I am wrong, that this room is wrong?" I cried.

He walked to the window, opened it, and stood staring down at the fading light on the canal, watching the slow passage of a barge.

I put down the brush I was holding. We were silent for some time.

"What can I give you? What can I ever give you? What can make it right for me, in my own mind?" His voice was soft, as though he spoke from very far away.

When was that? One day in March, one rainy March day in 1949. I looked at the river now, today, the Seine, the most romantic of rivers, I looked at the Seine and heard his voice all over again, recalling how even then it seemed very far away.

Now the taxi dropped me at the corner of the rue Meynardier. I looked around quickly for the café, the one on the corner where we used to meet. It is still there. It has not changed much, no neon lights, no copper fittings, none of the gadgets that seem to have cropped up all over this changing city. The walls are still covered with picture postcards. Only the man behind the bar is different. I ordered a coffee and looked at the postcards again. There were many more now, more than I remembered.

I walked up the street toward the canal. The houses seem much the same, a new one here and there, or a fancy filling station. But mostly the same. There is the shop where they sell tropical fish and worms and turtles. And there is the *boucherie chevaline* with the three remarkable horses' heads over it. I have a sketch of it somewhere.

"You are giving me something. Something that cannot be condemned by any Church. And that is love. God is love, don't they teach you that in Sunday school? God is love. And if circumstances are difficult and wars and poverty and misfortune prevent you from translating love into a legality, that is not necessarily your fault any more than it is mine!" I answered him.

"Translating love into a legality," he repeated, turning it over in his mind. "What a strange way you have of using words at times. Tell me something, Carola. Quite honestly. Do you believe in God?"

I looked at him, at his troubled eyes, and was afraid to answer. Afraid to hurt him, afraid above all of losing him.

The three handsome horses above the *boucherie chevaline* looked at me now in the evening light.

"I don't know," I answered.

"That means you do not."

"No. That means I don't know."

"But if you doubt it, if you doubt God's existence, what must you think of me? What can you think of me?" he said quietly, turning back to the window.

Could the three horses be laughing?

"I don't see the connection. Whether I believe in God or not has nothing to do with what you believe in or with anything else between us," I said.

"Of course it has. Don't be blind. Look. I am studying to be a priest. Yet I live here with you, make love to you, share a life with you, want even more than that, want even more than I have with you now—all the while I am studying to be a priest. Does that not strike you as contradictory? At least as contradictory?"

"Perhaps. In a way," I said slowly.

"Ah, at last! Well, then, what kind of an idiot must I be to allow myself to fall into this position? Either a sensualist or a hypocrite, a man of God who fornicates or a hypocrite who pretends to be a man of God. I don't know. And who are the other men of God? Who are the others I see? Those who keep me for months with a hunger so maddening that no thought of God can break through it, those whose bigotry is only greater than their stupidity, those who have learned their lessons by rote and have never questioned them since? Those who would condemn me for loving you and you for letting me love you? Oh . . . I don't know. I don't know anything any more." He sat down on the edge of the bed, tired.

"And if you don't believe in God how can you understand what I am . . . what I am trying to . . . "

"Look," I said, sitting down next to him. "I don't understand anything about your vocation. I don't even know whether that's the word for it. I don't know what makes a man different because he wants to serve his God, his notion of God, in being a poet or a cobbler or in being a priest. It all starts with you and it ends with you. As long as you are honest with yourself. I have no worries as to whether I am doing something wrong with you, here. I am not! Being legally married to you would not change a thing for me. But

80

I do admit, in a way, that all the rules of . . . of what? dogma? tell us no—marriage is a sacrament and the marriage act is for . . . for club members, if you like. But somewhere in God's famous mercy there must be some kind of rule that allows for people like us. Where love is real and beautiful and clean and where the world around is not just difficult but damned near impossible. Surely, Mihailo, yours is not a wrathful God who doesn't understand about love?"

He smiled at me, as one smiles at a child who is trying very hard, indulgently.

"No. He is not wrathful. But I am not sure He is as understanding as you think."

"Mihailo," I said to him after a few minutes. He was standing by the window again, staring down at the canal. "Mihailo. It's not wrong."

He turned to me, held me to him, gently stroked my hair. But he did not answer.

I have no curiosity today to see the church again. Passing the three splendid horses' heads, I will move on to the canal. There is a fine iron footbridge there, a Victorian drawbridge, which raises itself to let the barges pass. There used to be a metal sign on it with a picture of a horse and carriage and a warning: Trotting Forbidden on the Bridge.

Chapter Thirteen

THE locks of the canal were now before me, unchanged. Ghosts! Is that what I am doing, laying a ghost? But whose ghost, his or mine? Which broken child am I looking for? The girl who drifted into madness and then drifted out again because everyone around her told her it was the thing to do. Running away? The doctor, the mother, finally Gavin. Oh, yes, they were right, all of them; and she had stopped running away, except that she would never visit Paris because Paris was the one place where her new and permanent kind of running away would be found out. And she could not afford that. Was this the ghost, then? Her own? Or was she really prepared to lay that other? And are both of them so abstract to me now that I refer to myself in the third person and to Mihailo as "him"? I walk along the canal trying to put the pieces together, to find a reason in a web of absurdities.

The canal is unchanged, perhaps, but all around it the years show themselves. New and ugly houses, big ones, square ones, jerry-built ones, peeling and unpretty, seldom livened up by even a geranium in a window. The old ones, small and narrow, are still there, so northern in shape and tones of grey that I used to be surprised at finding French signs on the shops. This should be somewhere else, in some other country with a half-unknown language; Latvian, for instance. But not French.

I wondered, looking at the changes, at the amazing number of automobiles in Paris, at the freshly cleaned buildings and squares, at the prosperity manifested in good clothes, stout shoes, or expensively flimsy ones. I wondered how much a *carnet* of métro tickets cost now, how much it was then, in 1948. How much did a *carnet* cost in 1948? I cannot remember, yet I should know. Is this really Paris? Is there really such a place as Paris? Or was it Paris then? Is not Paris just an idea, a notion one forms of somewhere, anywhere, where one was very young and very innocent? Isn't that my idea of Paris, nothing to do with this noisy place full of cars and pushy, pushing people, where neon and copper have taken over the bistros of my imagination?

There is no Paris; there is a nameless place where youth lives and flourishes and dies, where all that takes place naturally and with ease, a land to which one does not return. Because it is no longer there. There is a line of Eluard's: "Hier c'est la jeunesse, Hier c'est la promesse". Yesterday is promise.

The railings are damp and there is a barge with a fine shiny wheel and behind it pots of ivy and a calendar.

A sturdy red-cheeked little boy is playing on the deck. The barge is passing in front of a tall grey house, a huge multi-storied thing with balconies. That is what is left of the tiny Hotel du Midi. Poor Jean, dead, too, and his little hotel a great big apartment house. Here is Paris, here it's not. It seems to fly in and out of my head, this non-existent Paris; now you see it, smell it, touch it, now you don't.

There on the third floor where I see nylon curtains and flowered drapes, right there was me. For nearly two years I lived there, I was there, I existed because it existed, it existed because we existed, because we breathed life into it, because Jean and Nicole had created it, had warmed it, had welcomed us, fed us, wrapped us in affection and laughter and joy. And now it is somewhere between the flowered draperies and the stairwell of a huge block of flats. And Jean is dead and Mihailo is vanished and I am just a little bit dead myself. But there it is.

Of course, the new café is called the Café du Nord and it is full of neon and copper and red and yellow appliqués on the wall.

A ham sandwich, please, and a *ballon de beaujolais*. Yes, on the terrace, please. No, it is not too cold. It is very warm for May.

How curious to search through one's mind, like sorting through furniture stored away, some of it unsightly, other pieces flooded with sunlight, bright and still new despite the years of shadows.

The Easter holidays of 1949. Everyone was going somewhere, everyone was getting ready to take a train, a bus, or to hitch-hike. Claude was undecided because his mother and step-father were undecided. They thought of coming to Paris but Fred had business in England. We hesitated. Philippe and his communal automobile, the only car any of us had access to, were going to Switzerland. Which was unfortunate.

"I just spoke to Mother," Claude said, out of breath from running up the stairs. "They're going to England. But we can go to Cannes anyway. Gaston in the village will have the key. Mihailo is more than welcome. She made it a point to say that, by the way. I'm afraid she's getting very romantic in her dotage. Anyway, we're off."

Claude and I waited for Mihailo at the little café on the rue Meynardier that Wednesday. The three of us made a funny picture in the spring rain, ignoring the rain, talking of sun and boats and the Côte d'Azur.

"How will we go? Three cannot hitch-hike at once," Mihailo pointed out.

"Oh, to hell with hitch-hiking. What with student re-ductions, the train will come out just as cheap. Don't worry about that. I'll pay for the ticket. You can pay me back later." Claude brushed it aside. I saw Mihailo colouring.

We went up to the room in the Hotel du Midi. Claude had never been there. "What an amazing view," he said, looking out the window. "Looks like Bruges in the rain."

Mihailo and I smiled at each other. It was like showing off one's baby, after all.

We drank slivovice, a Yugoslav plum brandy, while our shoes dried near the stove and we made plans for a fortnight in the sun.

It was still raining when we set off from the Gare de Lyon on the crowded night train. We woke up under a brilliant blue sky in sight of parasol pines and mimosa, and the sun was warmer than we expected it to be.

"There's nothing like a Paris spring to make you appreciate the Midi," said Claude.

"Unless it's a Paris winter," added Mihailo.

Lying on the beach on the hot sand, eating those incredible *salade niçoise* sandwiches, not swimming really because the water was cold, just lying there drinking in the sun, laughing or clowning on the sand, the days drifted by. We took buses here and there, Nice or Monte Carlo, to show Mihailo because he had never been there before. We had neither the clothes nor the money for the Casino, but we walked around the outside, "to get the feel of what luxury should be". We took long walks in the hills, we chatted with the neighbours who rolled their r's the way Mihailo did, only more so. We cooked intricate meals or else ate only sandwiches and scrambled eggs. We slept till noon or woke up at six "to take advantage of the time". We played music, we read, we did nothing, we did everything.

We drifted through the hills in the evenings, the perfumed hills of the Midi, the three of us slightly high, our arms linked, singing songs. A few more days in the sun, lunches on the beach, erratic dinners on the terrace, afternoon naps or hikes, a sail around the harbour, a visit to Eze, that medieval mountain perch, a last pastis in the port and a hasty scrubbing of the kitchen, then back to the night train, the three of us sleeping fitfully in the crowded third-class compartment, going north.

Chapter Fourteen

THE days grew warm in Paris. Mihailo arranged to be free most evenings. We were together more than before, before the Easter holiday.

I was invited to the opening of a Picasso exhibition at the Maison de la Pensée Française. We went to museums together, we stood in line again at the Ursulines, we heard Sartre at the Sorbonne, Camus, and Gary Davis, too. We heard jazz in small cellars near the Seine, we danced in Montmartre—along with all the other American tourists. We ate at the Cité Universitaire, we picnicked in the Bois de Boulogne. We discovered the parks of Paris, the lesser known ones, the Parc Montsouris and the Buttes Chaumont. We drank endless beers at the Flore, the Select, the Dome, the Coupole, and ate sandwiches on the quais of the Seine. We went to the top of the Eiffel Tower. Why not? We saw José Greco and his sophisticated Flamenco dancing, and listened to records of Pepe Pinto and La Niña de los Peines on the squeaky pick-up of a Spanish painter in Montrouge. We cheered the end of rationing that spring, we listened to lectures by Merleau-Ponty and John Steinbeck, we saw rehearsals at the Comédie Française, and Louis Jouvet doing Knock. We read, we listened, we talked, we dreamed.

We sailed through the weeks, no notion of time, nothing more pressing than the last métro to catch. We were without time, without frontiers, limitless, weightless.

The summer was near. We would go to Cannes again. Of course. Then we might hitch-hike down to Italy, go as far as Sicily, perhaps. Claude and I were talking over routes, cities, islands.

Mihailo shook his head. "I have a job for the summer."

We looked up at him, surprised. "A job?"

"Yes," he laughed, "a job."

I was hurt. He had not told me anything about a job.

"Doing what?" I asked.

"Digging ditches or something. Anyway, manual work in Germany."

He laughed at my surprise, reached out and put his arm around my shoulder. "Only for six weeks," he said, the way one talks to a child.

When we were alone he explained. "This way I will be able to save enough money to buy a winter coat and shoes and still have something saved for a few months more. My cousin Alex will be in Paris for a few days next week. He will arrange everything. He has contacts with several student work organisations in Germany. Last year he made 100,000 francs net in a labour camp near Cologne. It would be very foolish of me not to do it."

I could see that he was right, but I could not hide my disappointment.

"And I shall buy three white shirts," he laughed.

"One for each meal?" I asked.

The long, lovely summer....

"What shall I do?" I asked.

"It is only six weeks and you will be in Cannes with Claude getting very brown and doing lots of paintings out of doors and perhaps learning to cook indoors."

"Will you go with Alex, or alone?"

"I hope with him. But if not with him, with Serge, one of the boys from the seminary. By the way," he added with a funny smile, "Serge has seen you. He thinks you are very beautiful."

88

I looked up at him. "But I have never met Alex, have I?" Somehow, in the back of my mind, I knew that this Alex had not been told about me. I don't know how I knew, but I did know from the beginning that Alex was someone to be reckoned with.

"Well, he has been doing research in Heidelberg. He has an excellent scholarship. He is doing a thesis on Kierkegaard, but from a Christian point of view. All sorts of people are interested in him—Maritain, Gabriel Marcel..."

"That's only one sort," I interrupted. He laughed.

"Anyway, he's a brilliant fellow. You will meet him. Eventually."

Quite clearly, I was being hidden from Alex as carefully as I was hidden from the seminary people. And for the same reason.

"Eventually?" I gathered that Serge was a different type. I rather liked Serge.

"What are you smiling at?" he asked.

"Nothing. Am I smiling? Look! Seagulls!" And there were four seagulls over the locks, almost under our window.

How much was a métro ticket in 1948, why can't I remember?

The spring twilight warmed the terrace comfortably. I ate the sandwich watching the barges drift by. Seagulls. Now, too? Or are those pigeons today? I can't quite see.

Chapter Fifteen

THE fourteenth of July, 1949. Hot and sticky, we walked to the Bastille from here. Mihailo had on a T-shirt and dungarees, American surplus. I laughed at him because he looked like a cowboy, so big and rangy. He should not have been thin, his frame called for padding. "Tovaritch Cowboyski", I called him, and the day began and ended in laughter.

The Bastille parade, the great angry slogans of peace and friendship, down with this, up with that, incongruous Scots in kilts and bagpipes, how I wished they would play the Internationale on the bagpipes! Americans, Spaniards, everyone in the Bastille Day parade! We dropped coins in boxes and had ribbons and pins all over us. Peace was a fine word on a sunny day. And we walked and walked all over the city, no métros, no buses; we walked so we could see and hear everything on Bastille day, for revolutions were celebrated on foot.

We ate *frites* and hot dogs by the Seine, cheese and *baguettes* in the Square Louvois, nodding to the amazing statue of the four rivers of France. Someone had thoughtfully provided the Loire with a small French flag. We danced in the streets of the Île Saint-Louis, the tiny streets, seeing what a fourteenth of July was, what a Bastille day felt like. Smelling and touching, loving Paris, feeling Paris rise up in our throats and moisten our eyes, feeling each other's bodies dancing in the crowded, lantern-hung streets, holding each other's warm hands, kissing laughing mouths, late into the warm, music-filled night.

Someone asked me years later if I had taken part in the

political demonstrations on Bastille day and I laughed—laughed because of the beers and the red wine and the Camemberts and accordions, which was all I knew, and Mihailo laughing with me, his head thrown back dancing to a Paris accordion on a tiny Marais square, finally asleep in my arms near the Canal de l'Ourcq, circles under his eyes, his thick black hair on the pillow, like my children sleep, all the way through.

And the long severed summer began. His train left from the Gare de l'Est at two o'clock on the afternoon of July 16th. I agreed with him, with his decision to take the summer job. It would not have done any good for me to disagree. Mihailo was a very stubborn boy.

We stood there in that huge station, awkward, not saying much. In 1949 the Gare de l'Est seemed colder than the other stations, sinister in a way, presaging the destruction of the eastern part of France, of the German cities the trains were to pass through, hours from Paris. On July 16th the air was chilly and damp. It had rained all morning.

"You'll be able to buy a new raincoat," I said, fingering the worn edge of the sleeves, as he sometimes did himself.

"Carola. You will write, won't you? I will write to you in Cannes and if you decide to hitch-hike to Italy Claude's mother will keep the letters for you. But you will write, won't you?" he asked a second time.

I was very lazy about writing, he knew that. If I had had the money I would have telephoned or cabled Tor rather than write letters. As it was, I got by mostly on postcards. Mihailo disapproved of postcards as a means of communication.

"I'll write," I promised.

The train was called. We walked up to it, passing ill-dressed people, crowds of families speaking Slavic languages, herds of young German boys—where had they come from,

91

where were they going, those disinherited young Germans of 1949? We passed the inevitable rucksack-equipped, stout-booted young British hikers in khaki, with scarves around their necks and sweaters tied around their middles. Going to see where they had been a few years earlier, under different circumstances. I did not like the Gare de l'Est. It still smelled of war.

Mihailo, tall and thin, his radiant smile lighting up that moment for me.

"August 28th. Remember! And I will be so rich! Carola, forgive me." His eyes seemed to laugh and plead at the same time.

The train moved, he jumped on. I stood there feeling bereaved. Already.

I went back to the Hotel du Midi that afternoon, tired and dejected. There were one or two people in the café. Jean was sitting by the window reading a newspaper. He looked up as I entered.

"Well—he's gone?" he asked, smiling.

I flopped into a chair opposite him. "Gone."

"And you leave tomorrow?" he continued.

"That's right."

"And you will both be back at the end of August. Both of you?"

"Yes."

He was keeping the room locked up for me. I looked at him, wondering what would come next.

"Tell me something, Carola. Could Michel go to America with you?"

I must have shown my surprise, because he made an impatient gesture—that man was a collection of impatient gestures.

"Oh, I know what you think, only the bourgeois can live in America, all you artists with souls must come to Paris.

But that is a lot of nonsense. You are too young to see that now, but you will see it, eventually. What I want to know now is whether Michel could live in America, could work . . . you know, as a Russian curé."

I looked away from him, out of the café window to the canal. "I don't know. I suppose so. I don't know very much about curés, Russian or otherwise. . . . "

We sat silently for a few minutes. I noticed then the affection in his eyes, the affection of a middle-aged, childless man for two children whom he had come upon by chance in his new, disjointed life in Paris. Curious French hotel-keeper, neither thrifty nor inquisitive nor any of the other things he should have been according to tradition. Only impatient, impatient with interferences, impatient with "les emmerdements".

"I don't even know whether he wants to be a priest, really. I don't think he knows himself, any more."

"What would happen if the Russians found out he was here with you?" Jean asked.

"The Russians", as if it were Stalin or the Tsar, the NKVD and the Red Menace. But I did not laugh. Jean always referred to the seminary as "les Russes". It was difficult not to confuse Mihailo with the Berlin Blockade in Jean's conversation.

"I don't know. Expel him, perhaps. I don't know. You see, his father is a priest and his grandfather and everyone else, I gather. His mother is a poet, though, and an English scholar. She's translated several books of poetry into Russian or Bulgarian or something. That's why his English is so good. He learned it as a child. He's such a curious mixture of con-tradictions, Jean, so difficult for me to understand, to even come close to on some things. And we have had so little time. . . " I finished lamely.

"And, you are so young. You know, when I see kids like you wading through situations complicated enough for people twice your age, I get panic-stricken. How can you possibly judge? On what basis can you judge life? What do either of you know about anything, after all? Panic-stricken, that's what I get, panic-stricken! It takes so little, so little to make you do something silly, to put you off completely, for the rest of your lives."

He looked down at his empty coffee cup, his red face tender and kind.

Jean is dead now, and so is his hotel. Both are dead and I am sitting here on another terrace, a lifetime later, seeing his head bent over his coffee cup, hearing his rich southern voice, seeing from a cold distance what he saw then, so close.

The circle of light floods the canal, pierces my eyes, turning with certainty within my eyes, around the image of Jean, the image of his concern, his kindness and concern.

"Another Beaujolais, please. Tell me, how much was a carnet de métro in 1948, do you remember?"

But the waiter looked at me blankly, making me aware of my foreign accent, my odd question; he shrugged his shoulders and said, "I was seven years old in 1948, Madame," leaving the glass of wine alone on the table.

One Sunday night before that vacation Mihailo and Jean were sitting at a table in the café while I sketched them as absinthe drinkers.

Jean asked him brusquely, "How old were you when you went into the maquis?"

"Seventeen," Mihailo answered with a smile, guessing at Jean's reaction.

"Ah, pour des cons on est des cons!"

"Oh, come now, I would have been more of a con if I had stayed at home, wouldn't I? And think of the funny stories I can tell now! If I had stayed at school like a nice

94

little boy I would have nothing to talk about now. You understand.

"For instance. I was in a German prison camp in Yugoslavia, near Trieste. A buddy and I managed to get out. But we could not get out of the village, the roads were blocked. They had dogs, just to make sure. And we were terribly hungry—Carola laughs, all my stories begin and end with being hungry. Anyway, we hid in the cellar of a small house, the cellar door was open and we crept downstairs. There were potatoes in the cellar. We made a fire, a small fire on the dirt floor and we tried to roast them. It took ages, you can imagine. But we were so intent on roasting them that we forgot about the smoke; we didn't stop to think that the smoke might be noticed. The vision of the potatoes, big fat ones they were, was enough to make us forget everything. The poor potatoes had so many holes in them where we kept poking them to see if they were cooked that they looked like sponges after a while. Anyway, we were nursing the fire along with scraps of wood and paper when the cellar door flew open and we heard heavy steps on the stairs. The barrel of a rifle appeared around the bend.

"We stood up, terrified, and Dimi, my friend, whispered, 'Friend,' in Slovenian, which is what they speak there. Slowly, inch by inch, the rifle dropped. And around the bend in the stairs we could make out a huge form. My first idea was that of a bear. Dimi said later he thought it was several bears. It moved slowly into the light and we saw that it was a woman. But what a woman! Much taller than I, broader than both of us put together, wrapped up in gigantic folds of skirts and sweaters and shawls of different colours, different materials, layers of things, and from under the scarves around her neck we saw a remarkable face. A beautiful face, but insane. And dirty! We stood staring, transfixed. Then she motioned us to come closer. I turned and looked at the

95

potatoes, seeing them disappear from my reach—so close—they would burn. She must have noticed the way I looked at them. Then she let loose a huge, horrible, terrifying laugh and said in German, in a mad voice, 'The babies are hungry. Eat my babies, eat. . . .' She poked Dimi—both of us were thinner than the potatoes, if you poked us we fell—she jabbed him with her elbow and she began to sit down, to lower herself to the floor by the fire. Then she took a potato from the fire and handed it to Dimi, laughing insanely to herself.

"We were terrified. She was German, this monster, and she was without doubt insane. We juggled the potatoes in our fingers because they burned, but we began eating. Dimi and I did not dare to look at each other. Yet we were so hungry that eating came first. Hunger is even bigger than fear, I guess. We ate the potatoes, three each, all there were. She sat there rocking back and forth on the floor, watching us, cackling, making chicken noises, saying 'eat', but mostly making noises like an animal in her throat, her dirty face and crazy eyes watching us with pleasure. When the potatoes were finished I began to feel the fear I should have felt before. And Dimi! I looked at Dimi and I saw how he was looking at the woman. I saw how frightened he was—not frightened, more than that. Petrified, mesmerised. You know, the way a bird is mesmerised by a snake about to strike. And from the back of my mind I got the crazy idea that snakes like music. And slowly, without really thinking it out, I began to sing, very softly, low. And she swayed back and forth to the song, her crazy face wearing a smile that seemed almost beautiful under the dirt, under the shawls.

"I kept on singing, slow sweet nursery songs, for what seemed like an eternity, neither Dimi nor I moving, just watching her rock back and forth until she finally fell asleep. By then we had both regained enough presence of mind to move quietly, so as not to wake her, and we crept out of the cellar, up the steps and out of the house."

"My God," whispered Jean after a bit. "Then what happened?"

"Oh, we were picked up and sent to another prison camp. In Austria," Mihailo answered with a wave of his hand.

"And Dimi? What happened to him?"

"Ah, poor Dimi. I am afraid he is in prison now. We were together all the way through the liberation. Then I was sent to hospital in the British zone and Dimi went home in a convoy of partisans in late 1945. He finished at the university this year and was arrested shortly after. Along with a lot of others."

"On est cocu de tous les côtés dans cette histoire," mumbled Jean. "Screwed from all sides."

Mihailo shrugged his shoulders. "No more than anyone else," he said.

Jean made us ham sandwiches. It was late and the café was closed. We drank glasses of *gros rouge*, rough red wine, the three of us rather pensive.

Mihailo leaned back in his chair and said, "I would like to be a pig farmer. Like that I would always have a ham nearby." He said it dreamily, gazing at the sandwich in his hand, an expression of profound contentment on his face.

Jean and I burst out laughing.

The fading light on the canal plays tricks on my eyes. The Hotel du Midi is there opposite me, where it never was, and my curtains flap in the open window on the third floor. There is the easel, there is the painting, there is the fluffy blue blanket I bought—for if Mihailo was obsessed with hunger, I was always cold.

The hotel had few other tenants. Jean, not well physically even then, kept only those tenants he was forced to keep by

97

law, because they had been there when he bought the hotel. The others lived on the second floor. They smiled at us and we said hello, but there was no friendliness. Nor were they friendly with Jean. He would not let them be. One by one they left, and he refused to take more. He was tired of hotels, Nicole said. And what little money he had was all he needed. Nicole was often away, tending to a sick mother in the country, and Jean, his impatient gestures flung in the direction of the second floor. Jean had no more time left for tenants. Except us. Yet even then I think he knew we would not be there for long enough to help us all the way.

I can see them clearly now. They are pigeons, not seagulls. I have not seen any seagulls yet. Perhaps there are no more left in Paris.

Chapter Sixteen

WHAT happened to that summer? Nothing. It was a wonderful summer. Even though Mihailo was not with me, it was still a good summer. It was not a tragic age, after all.

Six weeks of holidays with Claude in Italy and the south of France was not a catastrophe. I spent my twenty-first birthday at the Casino in Cannes, with Claude and his parents, who took us to dinner at Eze, overlooking the sea. We hitch-hiked to Portofino, to Florence, to Rome. We read D.H. Lawrence and Compton Mackenzie and Axel Munthe. We ate in tiny trattorias on the Via Margutta with Art Students League expatriates. We saw the Pope, we swam at Ostia and hitched to Naples and then went to Capri and Ischia. We had a room with a view in Florence, or rather two rooms with two views, and two copies of Forster. We did not dare see Beerbohm, though Claude had a note to him from a friend of Fred's. We wandered through Cinecittá, full of beautiful girls and muscled young men undressed to play Hercules or slaves. We had no money left to go to Venice, which was a pity, but we ate a Florentine steak and took the train for Nice.

The warm August days brought the summer to a close, and as it closed around me I felt an unfamilar doubt. During the warm, thyme-scented nights in Cannes I felt a certain "trac" at seeing Mihailo again, a funny kind of fear, a stage fright. I thought of how he would look on the platform of the Gare de l'Est, how we would look at each other, the first awkward moves. It was not a solid love, it was a young love and uncertain in its certainties. We carried with us the awkwardness of adolescence, the vulnerability of young bodies, of unsure carriage. We had nothing more than what we were born with.

Days before he was to arrive I returned to Paris, roaming about nervously. I stayed in my room on the rue du Dragon. I did not go near the canals. I jumped from café to café, alone or with others, I went to endless movies, disjointedly, in my malaise.

At the station in Cannes Claude had bought me a copy of Simone de Beauvoir's *L'Invitée*, to read on the train. The book had a terrible effect on me. I was unreasonably depressed by it, by the young woman's acceptance of intrusion, of disaster, of death into her life. I read the book in spurts, putting it down furiously, indignantly, only to take it up again in anger an hour later. How could she *accept*? Why did she not fight! But at the very beginning! The word, the concept of *accepting* filled me with rebellion. The book haunted me in those days before Mihailo was to arrive, putting questions into my universe which were more troubling then, because they were only half understood, more troubling to me than the childish apprehensions I felt waiting for his return.

If I sit here on a chilly terrace fifteen years later, looking at myself, through myself, past myself to that boy who walked along the *quais* of this canal with me, the boy who brought me out of childhood to the age of reason, to the age of injustice and absurdity, to the age of acceptance, if I am here jn search of Mihailo, I am in search of myself. I am faced with the truth finally. That boy is no more, and the image I have borne within me of him has turned to an image of non-reality.

When Tor died and I had finished with the world which had been mine, I started not a search but a burial. Tor was dead and Mihailo had left me, refused me, had disappeared. I buried them both on the same day, uncomprehendingly, in raw graves. Yet it was from the moment of that burial that the search began. The years in New York, how long, how cold they seemed. Then Gavin, and with Gavin a restored life. I accepted him and what he offered, not a numbed, painless life but a full one with children and houses and head colds and bills and schedules and dogs and schools and summer holidays and friends and fights. But above all I accepted it, I learned how to accept. Yet all the time in a corner inside, in a private corner, there were that boy and that girl who had lived on a different plane; who lived still within me.

Chapter Seventeen

"IF you only knew," I wrote to him, "if you knew how afraid I am now. I can see you already."

The slow days drew themselves out, including a last interminable afternoon. The train was to arrive at six. I took a métro from the Odéon and watched the stations go by—Saint Michel, Châtelet, Etienne Marcel. How many can there be? As though I had never taken a métro before. But the métro arrived and I walked across the ugly station, and the train reached the smoky quai, my heart pounding away like an engine itself.

And there he was, walking toward me slowly, tall, not very tanned, and before either of us spoke he smiled, and I knew in that split second of a smile, before it ever reached his mouth, in the remarkable light of his eyes I knew. And in knowing, all the fears were shed and I breathed out for the first time for days, a huge breath of happiness, of joy, of laughter and joy. We were in each other's arms, tangled and warm and sure. So very sure!

Jean had put flowers in our room, big white daisies. Everything had been dusted and the window panes glistened. "Later on," he waved to us, "later on we'll have a drink and talk about les boches. Later on," waving us off on our own.

We looked at each other, alone in the bright room, shyly, eyes darting away to the window or the easel, phrases and voices sounding funny to each other's ears.

"I'd forgotten about your accent," I said, laughing a little, "how you roll your r's."

"And yours in French. The way you say 'à tout à l'heure'," he answered.

Then, looking at me from across the room, "How brown you are. Like an Aztec. An Aztec with gentle eyes." I walked past the easel to where he was standing, our eyes meeting timidly.

Soundless, wordless, timeless in each other's arms, his warm mouth on mine, my shoulders against his chest, my hands touching his neck, his face, his hair, the tender planes of his face. No longer timid, his strong arms crushing me to him, no longer shy but sure and knowing and young.

"Comme je t'aime, comme je t'aime, c'est la folie comme je t'aime."

September. There was a going-away party for Claude. My God, what a party! It lasted all weekend. We had not yet begun school, no one was in a rush. There was still a fragrance of holidays left in the air.

People started arriving at the rue des Saints-Pères flat on Friday evening. Who was there? Everyone. Painters, poets, the cinema crowd from the Montana, the Rose Rouge, the Tabou crowds, too, jazz musicians with their instruments, several South Americans with guitars and capes and maracas. People our age, others older, people we knew, others we knew of, still others we had never heard of. Monique and Fred came to Paris to see Claude off. Their friends came, too, more painters, older ones this time. Claude's friends from the Conservatoire, Philippe and half of IDHEC, the Cinémathèque people, dancers, actors, playwrights, pretty girls. Lots of pretty girls. Were parties different then? Were people less phoney, less superficial, less conscious of exteriors? Or was it because we were so young and the war was just over and somehow things were new again? Probably that. Yet the girls in their New-Look skirts and turtle-neck sweaters and exaggerated beads, the girls looked younger. There was an innocence in the frenzy of the early post-war years, an innocence in the hurry, the breath-taking haste to jump in, to know everything, to see everything, to try everything.

Early on Friday afternoon Claude and I started moving furniture out of the living-room, rolling rugs, sequestering anything breakable, and placing dozens of ashtrays all over the flat.

We were relaxing over tea with Monique and Fred when Monique said, off-handedly, "I'm going to meet the beau Slav, n'est-ce pas?" smiling at me. "I'm anxious to see if he is really as pretty as everyone says."

"Pretty? He's six feet two and undernourished. If you call that pretty, well, I know nothing about women," Claude barked.

"Jealous?" asked Fred, grinning under his untidy hair.

"Bloody grateful, on the contrary. Took her virginity off my conscience, he did. Imagine how difficult it was for me to have to worry about Carola's future, her id and her libido, in the middle of Saint Germain-des-Prés!"

"Ugh," I said, "if you're going to start on my virginity again. . . ."

"Lovely conversation," Monique interrupted.

"What is he going to do this year?" asked Fred, putting his cup down and taking a cigarette.

I was surprised that he asked. Fred never seemed very much aware of what went on around him. He was a tall, vague Englishman with an exquisite sense of humour and a calm that was reassuring in that rather upside-down household. I had never noticed that he paid much attention to anyone other than Monique.

"This year? Why, I suppose the same as last. I mean, I don't know. He only came back a few days ago. We haven't had much time to talk," I answered.

Claude snickered meaningfully.

"Oh, shut up. You're insufferable," I laughed at him, colouring.

"But does he still want to be a priest?" asked Monique, adding with a funny shudder, "How odd, the idea of a priest. Oh, I know the Orthodox are different, but somehow I wish they were called ministers or pastors or something less . . . less churchy."

"Very odd," I agreed.

"Surely, dear," continued Fred, "you are not thinking of . . . of anything, eh, definite? I mean, you know, marriage or something. . . ."

I looked down at my teacup. "No."

"The hell she isn't!" said Claude.

"I'm not!"

"Merde!"

"I'm not! Besides, we've never even discussed it. And anyway, wouldn't I look cute serving tea and *piroshki* to the *émigré* ladies of the congregation! And what congregation? Brisbane, Australia or someplace. No. If Mihailo becomes a priest—"and the idea crystallised in my mind for the first time, came out into the light, into a visible form for the very first time—"if Mihailo becomes a priest he does it without me."

But why? I said quietly, as though it were understood, as though it were not a new thought, a suddenly clear thought, a path to follow. Without me. There is no without me! Even as a priest in Brisbane, Australia. There is no without me!

"Carola, can I take a bath, too?"

"Sure. She'll never know the difference. She's too deaf."

"Are you sure? Supposing she saw me coming out?"

"Then she would surely not mind."

"No, I'm serious."

"So am I. O.K. I'll watch around corners for you."

"Ahh. I haven't had a real bath since Cologne."

"Don't tell me about it."

"Oh, how I miss baths. . . ."

"You probably eat in them."

"Who will go first?"

"Both."

"Both in the bath?"

"Tiens, that rhymes. . . ."

"Carola!"

"I'll scrub your back."

"She won't hear?"

"Were you planning to scream?"

"Wait. . . ."

"For what?"

"Till the water gets up to here."

"Ouf. . . . It's slippery! Hey!"

The group sitting by the fireplace was arguing heatedly about Yugoslavia.

"But if the Ustachis are the only ones in prison . . ."

"Oh, for Christ's sake, you people make me sick. Every goddam Jug wasn't a Ustachi . . ."

"A sacrifice is needed on the part of every citizen in a socialist state so that the system can be built out of the ashes of imperialism, feudalism, and war . . ."

"And if the neo-imperialistic Marshall Plan hadn't . . ."

"Now with Dewey sure to get in the White House for the next four years and with Roosevelt's ghost being banished further into . . ."

"You'll see how far Tito will go . . ."

"But Molotov said in his Kiev speech . . ."

"But these countries need communism. The people want communism . . ."

"Like Czechoslovakia, for instance . . ."

"Perhaps not. But Rumania, Hungary, and Yugoslavia especially, and Tito has . . ."

"But look at General Markos in Greece . . ."

"And if you saw Belgrade today . . ."

"Never mind about political prisons. It's a purge the country needs . . . blood-letting . . ."

"Sure! They didn't bleed enough for you during the war?"

"And Mihailovitch?"

"But it had to be that way. You can't be clement in a situation like that. If the Spanish Republic had cut down the generals in 1932 instead of pensioning them off. . . ."

"But Mihailovitch fought against the Germans before Tito . . ."

"Not before . . ."

"It was before, I tell you . . ."

They did not notice the tall dark boy standing by the window listening to them, looking at them with something akin to hopelessness in his eyes.

"So this is Mihailo. Come here, we can have a chat," Monique said, smiling and extending her hand to him. They went off to a relatively quiet corner. I followed them with my eyes and saw them laughing together, Mihailo talking rapidly, laughing, too; Monique leaning back, nodding her head, smiling, her eyes watching him kindly, watching the quick movements of his hands, his head.

"You know," I said to Claude, "in a way I hate this party. I really hate your going away!"

We were leaning over the piano, listening to an American Negro boy playing "Blue Moon".

"I'll be back at Christmas."

"And in between? You know, you're kind of like an anchor . . ."

"Zut!"

"You are!"

He laughed. "Well, you don't look as if you're about to drift out to sea without the Potemkin running after you, you know."

"Dope!"

"I know, I know. Actually, it's rather odd all the way round. London is going to seem . . . well, funny. Only not so funny. But what can I do? In a way I'm a bit of a displaced person myself, you know. After two years of coaching I still have an accent in French . . . despite place of birth and passport and all the rest."

We were silent for a few minutes, gazing down at the boy playing the piano. "The Darktown Strutters' Ball."

"Carola," he said after a while. "Look. If anything goes wrong, anything at all, you'll let me know? I mean, well . . . I mean, I don't know what I mean but you know . . ." and his funny crooked grin seemed to light up the whole room.

"I know."

"Oh, beware the infamous Pretzel," shouted Philippe from somewhere behind us. And there she was, pulling an embarrassed Mihailo from his corner with Monique, pulling him to his feet so he would dance with her.

She draped herself around him, a worm around a flagpole, running her hand up and down his back. He was laughing at her gently, but she was like glue.

"Allons libérer les Russes!" Philippe cried, off to war. But Pretzel clung fast to Mihailo's neck. It took a good long battle to disentangle her, the Left Bank's india-rubber woman.

"Don't make any noise. She won't hear us. She's fast asleep at this hour."

"But what will we do tomorrow morning?"

"Sleep late."

"But she will see me, surely."

"We'll pretend you've just arrived. Besides, tomorrow morning is an hour from now. It's five o'clock."

"She will make you leave if she finds I've spent the night here."

"Don't be silly. Shhhh."

"Ouf."

"You see? No problem."

"I'm too tired to undress even. Hey! What are you doing?"

"Helping ..."

"Good Lord!"

"No?"

"Well ..."

"If you are really too tired ..."

"Hmm?"

"If you are really too tired ..."

"Shhhh."

"Mihailo?"

"Hmmm?"

"Are people really ever too tired?"

"Sleep with your head here. Sleep, my angel, sleep. . . . "

Chapter Eighteen

"HE said no. No. Categorically. Out of the question. All the seminarians must live in. There is no exception to the rule."

"Oh."

The bishop, a beady-eyed old Russian, Bishop Ritoff. Mihailo had gone to him on October 2nd, when school was to begin, and asked him for an interview.

The night before in our room at the Hotel du Midi we had talked quietly for several hours.

"I will try to go on. You cannot understand what a disappointment it would be to my parents if I changed my mind for a reason they could not accept..."

"You mean for a reason you could not accept yourself," I interrupted.

"It comes down to the same thing. If I can accept a reason, so can they. They are both understanding, human. They would not ask the impossible of me. Let me try this year. Let me make sure. I will give myself this year. I am almost sure now, but I have to know for certain. I cannot let a decision as important as this be influenced by... by anything... what is the word?... extraneous."

I smiled.

"Don't laugh."

"I'm not laughing."

"So far all I have got out of the seminary is bitterness, hunger, and a loathing of hypocrisy. As well as a severe weakening in my faith... not in God, perhaps, but in everything He has created. How can I believe in the honesty of a man like Ritoff? How can I believe in the wormy old men who have no place to go and who come to the seminary because . . . not because they have a burning desire to serve God, but because they have nowhere else to go! And the hunger! And the filthy sheets, the smell of poverty and TB, of hypocrisy and pettiness. But I keep telling myself that all this is because it is in exile. If I were home, if it were home it would have been different, as it was for my father. Here, I must make allowances. I have to be able to cut away the bad wood, to see the core. I cannot discard what has been a certainty in my life ever since I was a small boy, I cannot decide quickly now, without . . . without care.

"Oh, and it is not all because of you. I have been disgusted from the very beginning. This is going to be the third year for me and for two years I have been on the verge of quitting. If I do quit now the decision will be independent of you. It would have been different if I had not wanted to be a priest. But I did! Very much. Only that seems like a long time ago."

He sat on the edge of the bed, his eyes far away. "But I am going to insist on living outside the dormitory. I will convince Ritoff somehow."

He did not convince Ritoff, however. On the contrary, that wily old Russian, smelling a rat, decided to change the programme for the new academic year. The students had to be in by twelve every night except weekends. We no longer had Wednesdays.

Everything changed. Claude left. We gave him a tearful send-off at the Gare du Nord, a crowd of us. Even Pretzel was downcast. I decided to give up my room at Madame Ferson's on the rue du Dragon. That is, Monique decided.

"Why pay rent, even if it is not very much, when you can have our flat? I will give you a key. Just keep your eye on things for me. Pay the bills, tip the concierge from time to time, and fix up the guest room for yourself, dust it once in a while, and water the plants. Cook that boy nourishing food as much as you can and as often as you can. He is too thin."

So I inherited the Gallien flat on the rue des Saints-Pères. But our room overlooking the canal at the top of the Hotel du Midi was home.

I used to meet Mihailo by the locks at five o'clock, and we would walk about during those autumn days.

As I am walking about now, aimlessly, looking at the canal, watching the changing lights, the passing of the barges, the games the children play.

The sun is hidden behind clouds now. I will walk faster because I am getting cold.

One is inexorably alone with injustice, with injustice inside, an ulcer, corrosive, burning through. There is no recourse. High on this iron footbridge, with the canal and its barges beneath me, flanked by warehouses, cranes, men moving among machines, coal heaps, crates, and trucks, standing high on this footbridge, a fine Paris rain beginning to fall, I am trying to meet myself. I am trying with the kind of concentration I recall using as a little girl trying to remember dates in history.

Who was Mihailo? It is not enough to say he once was here and is here no more. I cannot believe in that. I cannot make my mind work that clearly, make it understand.

The wound that I have carried about with me since that March of 1950 was another wound. I had been abandoned by Mihailo. He let me go to America and then dropped me. He did not answer my letters, he disappeared from sight. Claude could not find him, he did not want to be found, I thought. Oh, I thought! How many things did I think. At the time.

And abandoned, left, hurt, uncomprehending, I turned

in on myself, blindly accepting what I could not understand. There was no end put to my love for Mihailo because there was no reason to end it. No reason to stop, no way to put a final period to the line, no way to tell myself I must stop loving him, that I must accept the fact that I can no longer love him. How could I accept such a fact when facts as such have nothing to do with love? And what facts? There was only an absence of facts. There was only silence, a void. Where there should have been reason, dialogue, noise, even yelling or shouting, there was silence, there was nothing. I could not stop loving Mihailo; I have never stopped.

But I have become afraid of him, over the years. Afraid of myself and Mihailo, together. There is a question of lucidity. I refused to come to Paris because I was afraid. Overcoming Gavin's exasperation at my refusals, my elaborate and expensive alternatives to driving across France to get to Italy—I have made us go via every other less rational route imaginable—because I mistrusted myself. Because, perhaps, in the long run I did not want to know. Know what? Know anything. Know why he left me. Know, even, that he was here still, changed, grown into a man, a different man, know that perhaps I would not recognise him. Know, finally, that he had been woven into a dream of my own making, a hazy dream of odd patterns of tenderness.

But where was my lucidity? It wasn't. There was no lucidity. Here was a part of me exempt from lucidity, from analysis, from logic, from any degree of perception.

I have kept Mihailo to myself for all these years because... because I loved him as I have never loved anyone else, unquestioningly. Because I cast an image and he reflected it back to me; wholly, purely. Because we were one.

Chapter Nineteen

SCHOOL had started. The year had begun. I went back to the Grande Chaumière and took lessons from André Lhote as well. I was just as wrapped up in painting, in learning to paint, in seeing how others painted, as I was in the life around me. The new year—for years are measured from school time to school time, not according to calendars—the new year was different. I missed Claude terribly. Saint-Germain-des-Prés had lost most of its attraction for me without him.

Mihailo and I had a crazy routine worked out. We were together from five to midnight, or rather to eleven-thirty. If we found ourselves on the Left Bank I stayed overnight at the Gallien flat. If we were in the north, I stayed at the Hotel. I kept clothes in both places, but it was maddening for anyone as disorganised as I to fit things together easily. Whatever I seemed to be looking for was always at the other lace. Or so it appeared to me. I have no memories of those months without an image of myself carrying an over-sized bag on my arm, carting about sketch-books, extra shoes or sweaters, and a large assortment of keys.

Sometimes Mihailo and I would meet at the Select around six, or at the Café des États-Unis, which had become an artists' pub, full of people from the Grande Chaumière and from the many ateliers that abound in the 14th *arrondissement*. The atmosphere was different entirely from that of Saint-Germain-des-Prés. We used to eat at Chez Wadja, for next to nothing, or else at Roger la Frite. Where again? The Acropole, a little Greek place near the Boulevard Saint-

Michel. There were several little Balkan restaurants in the Latin Quarter, I suppose there are still, where a good meal would cost under forty cents. There was a Yugoslav one, too, with frescoes of Mihailovitch on the wall and a portrait of the King. Toward the end of the month we would eat in student canteens for sixty francs each, less than a dime. The meals, as I recall, were planned for bulk and iron content if nothing else. Lentils, I remember, were a serious part of student menus then, leaving me with an abiding horror of the things for the rest of my life. And *petit suisse*, a tasteless little turd of white cheese, and yoghurt, the merits of which Mihailo extolled from his Balkan childhood, but which I have never grown to like.

There was a little Greek pastry shop on the rue de la Huchette—Elliot Paul's street—where we used to buy small almond cakes for ten francs each, and we ate them on the street, powdered sugar billowing around us in clouds, on our faces and clothes.

Once in a while Tor would send me a package from home —tinned butter, corned beef hash, corn-on-the-cob in tins, ham, boned chicken, powdered soups, instant coffee, powdered milk from which we made thick creamy drinks at bed-time, Hershey bars, and Kleenex, cornflakes and Rice Krispies—all kinds of things which were either unfindable or unheard of in post-war Paris.

Whenever a package came it was a holiday. We would stack the goodies in two piles, one for the rue des Saints-Pères, the other for the hotel. Then we would proceed to have a feast. Mihailo often cooked dinner for us and for our friends. Garlicky dinners with lamb and rice and black olives, and lots of red wine. He was an imaginative cook, much more so than I.

He had saved most of the money he had earned during the summer. After buying a heavy duffle coat and a pair of stout shoes he rationed himself out seven thousand francs a month. With the three thousand the seminary gave him it brought the total up to ten. On ten thousand francs a month one did not starve, but neither did one eat well. Yet compared to the years before it was wild affluence.

The yellow Paris winter, damp and foggy, was upon us. The trek from the Left Bank to the seminary at night was both tiring and exasperating for Mihailo. We alternated, though, on no set pattern. There was more to pull us toward Montparnasse than to the canals, in one way. We had more friends there, there was more activity. Yet saying good night at the Vavin métro at eleven thirty was painful and irritating. The good bishop had not relented in his refusal to allow Mihailo to live out. On the contrary, he made it a point to check up on him. On Friday nights, to my intense annoyance, he inaugurated little get-togethers for the seminarians in his parlour, and he would speak to them of Holy Mother Russia and her glorious past.

The bishop, an unattractive man, had small eyes, shrewd and penetrating. Mihailo began to feel that the Friday night talks were a direct result of his request to live out. His impression was confirmed by Serge, who told him that one of the old men had intimated that Mihailo was the subject of considerable rumination on the part of the bishop and his priests. Why? Because this serious young man who had been docile and quiet had suddenly taken flight from them, though they did not understand why. And with only one year to go! Ritoff was not taking any chances with Mihailo. He was too precious a charge. Was not his father an eminent theologian, his great uncle an archbishop in St. Petersburg, his grandfather a noted church scholar? Ritoff's narrow eyes watched him carefully.

The result was that we spent more time on the métro than anywhere else.

Yet it was a gay time for us. Despite bishops and early trains to be caught, despite the lack of money and the cold weather, it was a time for laughter.

An American friend of mine opened a club in the Latin Quarter. It was a tiny cellar with a dozen tables and a bar. It was called the Blue Moon. But everyone called it Chez Aggie.

Aggie was a fiery little Negro girl from Washington who had a voice twice as big as her body, a charm and ease with people which made her an excellent entertainer, and one of the sharpest tongues in town. She hired a pianist and a three-piece combo and she sang herself. When business was good she brought in other singers. The show went on any time Aggie felt like it. She might sing three numbers or ten, depending on her mood. Her rich, powerful voice had nothing to do with the "college educated" jazz of the late fifties. She was strictly orthodox. I had met her with Claude when I first arrived in Paris. Oddly enough, she turned up as a pupil of André Lhote's. Aggie was a sensitive painter with an innate delicacy in her use of colour. Lhote was unusually interested in her work. We saw each other often, but did not become good friends until the winter of 1949, when she opened her club.

Mihailo and I dropped in now and then when we could afford two hundred francs for a beer. Although we made the beer last all evening, it was still a major expense. Aggie welcomed us with her own special brand of humour, and I became very attached to the place. She used to sketch her customers if she found them interesting. The back of the bar served as the "rogue's gallery", with quantities of pencil drawings hung every which way. She must have done a dozen sketches of Mihailo before Christmas that year. Tiny, with quick movements of her fingers, half his size, she would sit on a high stool at her bar, her lovely, mobile face intent on her drawing, intent on her swift fingers. "Man, has this boy got bone structure!" she would mumble appreciatively.

One night Mihailo did not come to the Select at six as he was supposed to. I waited until after seven, then walked down to the Gallien flat in case he called. But he did not call. Around midnight I went to sleep, uneasy but not worried. The next morning at eight thirty Jean phoned from the hotel. I could hardly understand him on the phone, between his southern accent and his agitation. One of the "Russians", a priest it seemed, had been in to see him the previous evening, to inquire about Mihailo's frequent comings and goings in the hotel. Jean, who was a good anti-cleric under normal circumstances, had developed a nearly pathological dislike of Mihailo's "Russians". He was almost apoplectic with rage. Fortunately, Nicole was there at the time, and she told the startled priest that Mihailo came there to eat, that was all. The priest then asked about the young American lady who accompanied him. That was his downfall. Jean lost all control and put the man out bodily.

I felt my heart sink. Mihailo's time of decision had come, and in the wrong way. I was near to tears. This was not the way to decide. These were not the grounds for decision. They must not put him up against a wall like this. He should be able to come to this coldly, not in anger. Not because of me, not because those bigoted people chose to close in on him.

I did not go to school that day, hoping he would call during the morning to tell me what was happening. But he did not call. At noon I crossed Paris by métro and went to the hotel. Jean was busy with customers at the bar. He waved to me and made a gesture telling me he would be up as soon as he could. I went straight upstairs to our room. A few minutes later there was a knock on the door. I shouted out "Entrez", thinking it would be either Jean or Nicole. But it was Mihailo and another boy, surrounded by several pieces of luggage.

That is, one battered suitcase and an assortment of odd packages. We stared at each other for a second, not saying anything. Slowly, he began to smile, until the smile on reaching his eyes seemed to light up the hall we were standing in, as though a huge new sun had risen around us.

"This is Serge." And then all at once the three of us burst out laughing.

"What is done is done. If they had not been so stupid I would still be there, trying to make up my mind, trying to rationalise, trying to justify them in my own eyes." Shadows played on his mobile face. He was sitting on the creaky pouf, Serge straddled a chair, and I was moving about the room restlessly. I see the three of us, suddenly so serious, so young. The pale December afternoon had faded, it was almost dark.

We celebrated what Serge called the Liberation of Mihailo with a bottle of some kind of cheap *mousseux*, fake champagne. It was Serge's gift.

They told me of how Ritoff had called Mihailo into his office, had threatened to write to his father exposing Mihailo's "scandalous conduct" in Paris, of how he claimed he knew all about the American woman, all about the infamous hotel, all about everything. If Mihailo did not repudiate this "liaison", Ritoff announced, his scholarship would come to an end and he would be expelled. "Think of the shock to your parents!" he warned. Whereupon Mihailo, who had been listening quietly to the old man's diatribe up to then, lost his temper.

He never told me what he answered or what actually did happen after that, but it was as if all the doubts in his mind had been dissipated for him, as though blown away by Ritoff's foul breath. All the excuses Mihailo had invented for Ritoff, for the seminary, for the basic dishonesty surrounding it, for the ugliness and hypocrisy—all the rationalisations he had armed himself with—all these were suddenly valueless. In his own mind the decision was made, and it was irrevocable.

He slammed the door of Ritoff's office, packed his clothes and books, amid the astonished stares of the others in the dormitory, and left.

Once the break was made Mihailo seemed to breathe more easily. I don't know how well I understood the torments he must have gone through that fall. I was so ill-equipped to appreciate them. The Orthodox Church seemed an odd mixture of liberalism and medievalism, nearly impossible for me to grasp. I was sorely unversed in dogma of any kind. I was almost embarrassed by the presence of faith or love of God which translated itself into a desire to become a priest. And my confusion was compounded by the exotic quality of the Orthodox Church. I am appalled at the extent of my ignorance now.

I was, of course, infinitely relieved that it was "all over", yet I was suspicious of any decision reached by Mihailo in anger. He was not an angry young man. He came slowly to anger, mistrusted it. More important still, and more indefinable to me at the time, was an instinctive conviction in my own mind that Mihailo was giving up an intrinsic part of himself, a part that he would have immense pain in remoulding into another form.

I had moments of fear at my own responsibility in this decision, a kind of helpless panic. But not strong enough; obviously, not strong enough.

Chapter Twenty

CHRISTMAS, 1949. Tor sent me a hundred dollars. We were rich! Millionaires! We would go to London, of course. I wrote to Claude asking him to find us the cheapest bed-and-breakfast in town, asking him to change his plans and stay there for Christmas and we would all come back for New Year's Eve together. Claude was delighted.

The idea of spending Christmas in London was marvellous for me. I love Christmas trees, snow, and Santa Claus, all the Anglo-Saxon trimmings. The French do not understand about these details, or at least they didn't in those years. Perhaps American influence and the Galeries Lafayette have changed France now. Then, however, the Yuletide spirit was still an English domain, and despite austerity, despite rations and clothing coupons, endless queues for second-rate food, plus a cold, damp winter, despite all that and much more, London was glorious at Christmas time.

Claude met us at Victoria, wrapped up to his red ears in a huge overcoat. "Steerage passengers this way," we heard him shout, even before we had spotted him on the platform. Then the two of us, mixed up in scarves and coats, were head and shoulders in a woolly embrace, Mihailo standing to one side. "Enough, enough, what will the English say," he grinned, separating us with a gentle tug.

"Salut, mon gros. I've arranged a London fog for you."

We walked through the icy station into a foggy, damp, luminous London, the three of us talking at once.

Our room was off the Cromwell Road, in a boarding house run by a Mrs. Mackenzie. Claude described her as

Kensington's Madame Ferson. She was just as deaf. We were shown into the room, and even that looked like Madame Ferson's—only in chintz and colder. Claude showed us how to work the shilling-hungry gas fire, and we all agreed that no one had ever exaggerated in literature or conversation about the British bedroom.

Walking along the Kensington High Street, with houses so familiar to a New Yorker, I was suddenly struck by the beauty of London, by the grace of English houses, English proportions, by the quality of craftsmanship in details—lettering on shops, fanlights, mouldings, gateposts.

"London is beautiful!" I cried.

Claude looked at me surprised. "Beautiful? No, do you think so?"

"Well, don't you?"

"No. Not beautiful. Paris is beautiful, Florence is beautiful. London is imposing."

Mihailo disagreed. "Beauty is not necessarily a feminine attribute, the way you apply it to a city. London's impressiveness, its grandeur, even its ugliness in some respects, is in itself a beauty. Not only Westminster which is obviously beautiful, but in the ensemble." It was a point we argued for days after. The more we saw of London the more beautiful it became. Even with the fog!

Claude had everything arranged. During the day we were to sight-see on our own. He still had classes, but had made out the most amazingly detailed itineraries, including his own comments, so that we had the feeling he was there at every step. The British Museum (no American should miss the Magna Carta and the Elgin Marbles—what would your mother say?), the Tower of London, the Houses of Parliament, Westminster Hall, the Victoria and Albert, the Dickens Museum, a literary trek through Hampstead, on to the Vale of Health (so quaint, my dear, so quaint), on to Bosworth

Field (and your friend Richard III), Petticoat Lane, Portobello Road, Waterloo Bridge (you know, Robert Taylor and Vivian Leigh and all that), the Tate and all those funny modern people, the National Gallery (they've got a Dutchman you might like), Buckingham Palace and Whitehall (if you had been more reasonable about George III . . .), Bloomsbury (looking for ghosts?) and on and on. We walked our icy feet off, relaxing in the clubby atmosphere of the tube, climbing up to the top of the buses, ducking into matinées because it was raining and because it has always seemed rather sinful to me to go to the theatre in the afternoon.

In the evenings Claude had other plans. A poor man's introduction to pubology. Mihailo was entranced by the pubs, those uniquely English institutions comparable to no other country's bars. Claude, an eminent pubologist, took us to dozens, all different, all with character, lives of their own. Then came the basic courses in modern drama—that was free tickets to plays his friends were appearing in. Then "an introduction to the Stately Homes of England", which was visits to his friends' flats—usually bed-sitters, filled with empty beer or wine bottles and peopled by the London counterparts of Saint-Germain-des-Prés. We got to know Soho street by street, doorway by doorway, pub by pub.

Christmas dinner was the three of us in Claude's room in Bloomsbury, near the British Museum. We ate kippers and drank a substantial quantity of Guinness, making blood-brother promises never to tell Monique and Fred that we had not had a proper Christmas dinner.

I suppose that it is because London has become so familiar to me now that the memory of that Christmas week has gone vague and confused in my mind. Long afterwards, when I settled here with Gavin and the children, I determined to forget that week in 1949. I was determined to refuse to see any traces of Mihailo in London, determined to discover the city as though I had never visited it before.

Years later, quite by accident, I came upon the crescent where Mrs. Mackenzie's boarding house once stood. There is a school there now. I felt a familiar pain surge through me, then a numbness, more familiar still. There was no more Mihailo in London anywhere after that.

We returned to Paris on the thirtieth, in time for New Year's Eve on the rue des Saints-Pères. It was a huge, formless, Claude sort of party, which went on well into the next day. It is odd to think of all the people around us as having lived on outside the static immobility of my memory of them, lived on outside my vision of them, making lives beyond the warm circle of Saint-Germain-des-Prés as it was then and as it certainly is no more. Boys like Philippe. Do they go to offices from nine to six, do they have children and mothers-in-law, do they walk their dogs at night? Do they sit at the Café Flore now, unaware of the change these fifteen years have wrought? Do they remember their faces and hands of 1948 as I do, fixed in a single image?

I suppose not. I suppose there was no cleavage for them as there was for me. I suppose . . . I suppose . . . I suppose . . .

There seems little left for me to do but to weave in and out of this unreality, a visitor from earth ill-at-ease in the Martian Paris of today.

Chapter Twenty-One

H<small>E</small> was standing by the easel, near the kerosene stove which did its best to heat the big, drafty room. The painting was a new one. I was trying to do something with the greys and blues of the canal, the cindery shades of the houses under that curious winter light. He squinted at it, screwing up his eyes to make the colours blur.

"I like that. I'm sorry you did not show him that one."

I looked up surprised. "This one?"

There was to be a group show at a gallery near the rue Bonaparte, a show of young Americans in Paris. My friend Teddy Klein, a round little painter from the Chicago Art Institute, told me about it. He was going to have something in it. Teddy liked my work, we had known each other ever since I had come to the Grande Chaumière. He claimed to like my work despite the fact that he firmly believed women painters to be a contradiction in terms. But contradiction or not, he was interested in what I was doing and arranged for me to show three paintings to the gallery-owner. If the man was impressed, then he would come up to my atelier— the room in the Hotel du Midi had suddenly become an atelier—and he would decide whether he would include me in the show. Apparently he did not want more than nine painters, and he had eight already. There was a vague chance.

I was very hesitant. Teddy was the one who was enthusiastic.

"Why not?" he pressed me. "What have you got to lose? I think your stuff is good, why shouldn't he?"

We were sitting in the Coupole, the two of us. I had no answer for him. He was right, after all. Why not?

"Look," said Teddy, "I'll come to your studio and help select what to show him. Then you and I and Mihailo can carry over three canvases. If he doesn't like them it hasn't even cost us cab fare. We can walk to the gallery from the rue des Saints-Pères."

"Oh, I don't paint there. I mean . . . I have a sort of studio up near the Buttes Chaumont," and I could feel myself colouring.

Teddy looked up at me sharply, then smiled and shrugged his shoulders. "OK. So it costs us cab fare. What's money?"

We walked down to the gallery and Teddy introduced me to the secretary; Monsieur Brunet was out at the time. The secretary made an appointment for the next afternoon, and we left.

"Come on up to what we now call my studio and you can see the paintings," I suggested.

"No, I'll come tomorrow, and we can bring three paintings straight away here. That is, if I ever find where the Buttes Chaumont is," he laughed.

The next day I was surprised by my own nervousness. I had been telling myself that the whole thing was a product of Teddy's natural ebullience, that there were hundreds of Americans in Paris much older and more experienced than I, not to mention better painters, and that the chances that this professional gallery owner would take a twenty-one-year-old unknown girl's work were about a billion to one. And I was not going to be excited about it! But I was a nervous wreck by the time Teddy arrived.

He came into the room full of stories of how he had got lost a dozen times, and expected Jean Gabin to come out of a room on the second floor, with a pre-war Gauloise stuck in his mouth.

Mihailo and I laughed at him. The hotel had become so familiar to us that we were amused at an outsider's reaction.

We went through the canvases carefully. Teddy picked out three, one of which I did not like. We argued about it but he insisted. That made me even more nervous.

We finally got ourselves into a taxi, canvases and all, and an eternity later we were dropped off at the gallery near the rue Bonaparte.

Monsieur Brunet was on the telephone. He talked rapidly into the receiver, smiling at us, waving at Teddy and eyeing Mihailo with undisguised interest. My heart sank. He made small, dancing movements, almost imperceptible, but he was all movement and fluidity, talking on the telephone. I stood there holding onto a canvas, not moving at all, feeling naked and chilled. The gaiety of the man's voice almost made me cry.

His conversation over, he crossed the room to greet us, his hand outstretched. Like a dancer, I thought. Yet he was all friendliness and ease. We propped the paintings against the wall and he looked at them; with kindness, I remember thinking. One was a much-stylised view of Paris roofs in ochres, greys, and blues; another was a composition of the hills near Cannes; the third was a portrait of Mihailo, sitting at a table.

My work was quite unformed; the only value it had, I suppose, was a certain delicacy of colour and a boundless admiration for Picasso. Monsieur Brunet looked at the canvases for a while, going from one to another, his hands in constant movement—now cupping his chin, again brushing through his hair, then touching his lapels, always in movement. I watched him fascinated, no longer nervous about the paintings, too interested in the personage, gratefully forgetting to be worried about his reaction.

"How old are you, mademoiselle?" he asked.

"Twenty-one, monsieur," I answered, trying hard to keep a laugh out of my voice.

"Twenty-one. Twenty-one. How marvellous to be twenty-one. How you make us feel your youth, mademoiselle!" I looked at him amazed.

"May I suggest that you show this portrait," he continued. "Or have you other things in your atelier that you are more interested in?"

Teddy, his round eyes popping from me to Brunet and back, answered first. I was suddenly struck dumb. Teddy talked to Brunet affably, comfortably, as though it were a perfectly natural thing that he should like the paintings and want them in his show, a perfectly natural thing, as though we were expecting nothing less. I did not dare look at Mihailo, though I heard him talking, too. They arranged the appointment for the next afternoon, we shook hands, I managed to say thank you and goodbye, but I was still in a state of shock when we reached the sidewalk.

Once out of sight of the gallery, Teddy let out a warwhoop. "He liked it! He liked it! You're the ninth American, Carola, you're the ninth American!"

Paintings and all, we walked over to the Flore and treated ourselves to Calvados all round. Pascal brought us over some writing paper and envelopes, and I wrote off two notes, one to Tor and the other to Claude, announcing the miraculous news that I was to have a painting in a Paris show. And what a show! Nine Americans in Paris!

Brunet came to the Hotel the next day, dapper and talkative, making much of my originality in living near the abattoirs. Such wonderful restaurants. He was most amused at the room and at my enthusiasm for the view. Some time later I learned that he lived on the Quai aux Fleurs, overlooking Notre-Dame. My view of the canal must have seemed curious to him indeed.

But he was a good-natured chap, and he did not press the point. He chose three paintings, two studies of the canals and the same portrait of Mihailo that had interested him the day before.

"The young man has an interesting head. Does he paint, too?" he asked.

"No." I answered.

"What does he do? Surely he is a student?"

"Yes. But he has just changed faculties. He is planning to register at the Sorbonne to do a degree in letters. But right now he's all mixed up with bureaucracy, I'm afraid."

"Ah, yes. One knows what that is. So many papers, so much time wasted. So depressing," he sighed.

In some ways he was too good to be true. Yet he was charming. He took the three canvases under his arm, chatting with me pleasantly all the time, asking me to drop in at the gallery to give him an autobiographical sketch for the catalogue. Gracefully manipulating the cumbersome paintings, he managed to extend his hand—again with the movement of a dancer—and off he went.

In one way I was almost grateful for Brunet's exoticism. It took my mind off the "serious" side of the story. Paintings of mine in a show? All I had to do was think of it and my head went reeling. One minute we had been outside the gallery rehearsing what to say to Brunet and how to say it, and the next minute I was IN. The comic relief provided by Brunet's mannerisms was welcome under those circumstances. I'll start taking myself for a painter soon, I scolded.

But it was not only me. It was all the others, too. None of us had ever showed before in Paris; most of us had never showed anywhere, for that matter. None of us was over thirty, several were under twenty-five. Brunet had an impresario's instinct for publicity. He advertised, he made noise, he put up posters, he put out feelers, he paid for articles here and there. By the time the show was to open there was a wide interest in the nine young Americans, long before anyone had seen a single painting.

The private view, he assured us, was going to be the first one worth the thirties. With his stage manager's touch, he got hold of most of the French film people who had spent the war years in America and had a "sentimental debt" to it. One never realised how many beautiful French actresses had been in Hollywood during the war until that February 12th. He even managed to rope in Lincoln.

Brunet told us we could invite as many people as we wanted. If the other eight had gone as dotty as I, the little gallery would have sunk into the river beds! I sent out nearly fifty invitations.

In the weeks before the opening, Mihailo was running around to a variety of students' affairs offices, university registrars, government ministries, and refugee centres, trying to get himself admitted to the Faculté des Lettres and—more difficult still—trying to get a student grant to cover his expenses. Universities are free in France. Food is not. If he were admitted to the Sorbonne, to the Faculty of Letters, in the middle of the academic year—a feat nearly impossible in itself—he was still not sure of getting his grant until the new term began in October. As a refugee he found things both easier and more complicated. He spent days at the Entr'aide Universitaire, the French government office which handles these matters. After endless waiting, they managed to get a transcript of his record from the seminary. That done, the Entr'aide promised they would speed up matters as much as they could. Then came the Sorbonne. He could only register as an "auditeur libre", not as a student working for a degree. Not until October, that is. Without proper Sorbonne entrance he could not qualify for a student grant.

Perhaps the refugee organisations could help? The Sorbonne people sent him to several refugee organisations, governmental, non-governmental, religious, non-denominational, non-profit, international, all of them with interchangeable alphabet-soup names, all with good will and good faith, and all with endless waiting lists. One woman asked him if he were a "hard-core" case. He told her he was not sure what that meant.

"Oh, you know, penniless, jobless, homeless, sick—that sort of thing."

He did his best not to laugh at her, at her IBM classifications of the different degrees of misery and her own pigeonholes of help which corresponded to them; pieces in an interlocking jigsaw puzzle.

"No, I don't think I am," he replied, still without laughing.

"Sorry, then," she had replied affably. "We only do hard cores."

"It was not even Kafka," Mihailo said shaking his head. "Or if you like, it is Kafka with computer machines. Hard cores here, soft ones there, everything neatly arranged according to your particular madness. Someone else asked me if I were a trade unionist. Because there was an opening in I-don't-know-where for a trade unionist in exile; if I could leave immediately, of course. Another told me to try Geneva. What does that mean? Try Geneva for what?"

"It's incredible," I said, listening to him.

"It's more than incredible. It's terrifying. The more offices I go to, the less conclusive the answers become. The only real answer is to wait for October and the new term. They suggest that I keep on at the Sorbonne as an 'auditeur libre' until then, but when it comes to the grant they shrug their shoulders in that infuriating Gallic gesture—'Ah, ça, monsieur. . .'—and as a last resort they say, 'Try the refugee organisations, perhaps.' Merde!"

But, hopeless as the situation was, we put anger out of our heads for the moment. The show was to open the next evening at six. We were too excited to think of anything else. Tor had sent a cable of congratulations, and Claude another, addressed to Marie Laurencin Thorpe. I bought a new dress for the occasion, a light tweed with a low scoop neck and long sleeves. It was beautifully cut, rather tight across the chest. I felt tall and thin and imagined I looked like Lauren Bacall. Which, of course, I did not. But it was a satisfactory illusion for an occasion as important as this. Mihailo's eyes twinkled as he watched me comb my hair, making sure it fell slightly over one eye. He smiled as I pencilled my eyes carefully, and as I took pains to put on my lipstick with a brush. He was kind enough not to say anything more than "How lovely you are" when it was all over and I stood in front of him for inspection. "And with heels, how tall!"

Teddy Klein and his friend Bob Andrews, another one of the nine, were coming up to the atelier for a drink and a snack before the show. Neither of them had ever seen the canals; Mihailo took them for a walk while I dressed. They waited for us down in the café, where Jean and Nicole had prepared a huge platter of patés and cheese and bread and butter. They talked enthusiastically about the canal, about the whole area, the lights and shadows which were so different, so alien to the rest of Paris. Jean and Nicole, amused at their French, just as excited as I was about the opening, had closed the café in order to be able to "concentrate", as Jean put it. He concentrated on Teddy and Bob, he concentrated on the exposition of his collection of drawings and oils, which he had hung ceremoniously all over the café along with a poster of the show in the middle, and he concentrated on getting us all a little drunk. We left the café around five. Jean and Nicole were to come along a bit later.

Crossing Paris, Mihailo close to me in the crowded métro, smiling down at me, both of us nervous, both of us feeling wordlessly that this was somehow jumping into an adult world, a giant step taken as though by magic.

"You're all grown up now," he whispered, his head bent over mine in the métro. "Look what you've done—showing in the first exhibition of young Americans in Paris since the war. And the only girl, at that! Oh yes, all grown up."

How close I held him, crossing Paris.

Better than Brunet had imagined it, more crowded, noisier, more replete with names to drop later on; the private view was a fantastic sucecss.

It was just after six when we arrived, and the gallery was full already. The actresses, gratitude to America in their hearts, no doubt, arrived in haute couture clothes and chauffeured American cars. The business men, the collectors, the befurred ladies who just adore modern art, the bejewelled young men who surely did something interesting in life, the half-dozen critics who counted, the smattering of real names who came for the right reasons, they were there, too. And all the Saint-Germain-des-Prés intelligentsia. And all the Montparnasse buddies of the nine painters. Dungarees and floppy sweaters, girls in black stockings and ladies in minks, the mid-western accents of the Embassy people and the velvety tones of the Crillon bar or the Espadon, cigarette holders and Gauloises Bleues, Jean Cocteau and the owners of the Hotel du Midi. It was quite an opening. Photographers flashed bulbs, my picture was taken by Mihailo's portrait, little red stars were glued to the paintings, the French radio held microphones in front of our faces and giggled over our mistakes in French. Aggie came with her three musicians, grinning happily at me and said, "Barnum and Bailey," nothing else. Philippe and Pretzel and others followed, whispered that we would all meet at Aggie's club later—

"Unless they take you to Maxim's, that is." Two tiny red stars were glued to my canvases.

Brunet sold out most of the show at the opening. The paintings were low-priced, but to us they represented fortunes. Teddy and I, half appalled, half enchanted, had our picture taken together. It went on until well after ten o'clock. The ladies, the cars, the polished young men, the names, the dungarees, the cigarette holders and the Gauloises Bleues cleared away, and our impresario, our own circus master, Monsieur Brunet, unruffled and calm, happiness surrounding him, lowered the lights and began to close up. I recall feeling at the time that it was a great pity Tor could not have seen it. It would have amused him enormously.

We took a taxi to the Latin Quarter. "People in our income bracket, you understand," said Teddy, leaning back in the cab, visibly moved by the sale of his three paintings, "people in our income bracket have a duty to the working classes. I have a personal duty to this cab driver's family, therefore I will pay the fare." Bernard Baruch.

Aggie's club was crowded, too. There were the usual Americans from the Grande Chaumière, the Montparnasse Spaniards—also painters—several Israelis who were romantic types with sonorous names and amazing stories of their recent war; there were young photographers with their ever-present boxes and cases flopping over their shoulders, and there were half a dozen American Negro jazz musicians who took turns providing the music.

Tables were arranged every which way that night. It was a private party. Anyone who did not know the others would probably have fled, that's how private it looked. We kept pushing the tables back to make the tiny dance floor bigger. Aggie sat on the piano, sometimes singing, sometimes just watching.

I was dancing with one of the Catalans very late in the

evening when I saw Mihailo walk over from the bar toward me, his eyes on mine, a quiet smile lighting up his face, his eyes reaching across the smoky room toward me. He tapped Jordi on the shoulder—"May I?"—and held me close, very close to him, dancing to "Les Feuilles Mortes".

"I like this song. I wanted to have you close to me. You do not mind?"

How often through the years I have seen him crossing that crowded floor, his eyes on mine, his eyes holding me to him for the rest of my life.

Chapter Twenty-Two

THAT was February 12th. It is inconceivable to me, even now, that within a month everything would be over, everything shattered, the pieces of our lives, of our love, strewn every which way.

Those early weeks of 1950, cold and foggy under Paris's yellow winter light, went by shapelessly, soundlessly.

Monique and Fred rented their flat on the rue des Saints-Pères, so I moved into the Hotel du Midi for good. I went to the Grande Chaumière regularly, but seldom early. After several frustrating, pointless weeks of trying to get his papers in order, Mihailo finally gave up for that semester. He had to wait until October, that was all. In the meantime he gave Russian lessons, tutored *langues orientales* students.

Serge dropped in to see us at the hotel with letters from Mihailo's parents, and news of the seminary. Each time he told of Bishop Ritoff's anger at Mihailo's leaving, an anger which seemed to grow, to feed on itself, rather than to fade with time. Mihailo would look at Serge as he talked, stiffly, saying nothing in return.

Leaving the seminary was more than just walking out. He had made the break under conditions which he found unacceptable to himself. He had never wanted to leave in anger. In a way, it was as though he had been cheated of making the decision himself. He resented Ritoff for having brought him to that point.

For weeks he avoided writing his parents about it. When he did, after Christmas, his letter mirrored the sorrow he felt in how the break came, rather than in why. He was understandably nervous about his father's reaction; his respect and affection for his father were boundless. He recoiled against the idea of hurting him. Days after the letter was written I saw it still in his pocket; he was unable to bring himself to post it. He looked at me rather sheepishly when he saw that I had noticed the letter, and that afternoon, passing the post office on the rue de l'Université, he took it out of his pocket, bought a stamp, and shoved it into the "abroad" slot, his jaw set and his eyes troubled.

For two weeks he waited for a reply. He did not discuss it, he did not seem to want to talk about it any more. At least not to me.

Then Serge arrived with the reply. Mihailo looked at the envelope with apprehension. He walked over to the window, staring down at the letter in his hand. Serge and I pretended not to notice; we talked about something else. Slowly, after a minute, Mihailo's face cleared and I saw his shoulders relax.

"It's all right. He says I did right. He says he understands." The relief on his face was wonderful to see. Serge looked at me and breathed out, showing me with a wordless gesture that it had been a close call.

My own curious relationship with my father made it difficult for me to understand Mihailo's relationship with his. If I had gone looking, I could never have found anyone as far removed from my own background as Mihailo. I had felt hopelessly inadequate during that fortnight of waiting. All I could offer now was my mute joy that he was once again at peace with himself and with his parents.

"Under other conditions, at another time, I might have judged you. However, in exile, in want and alone, as I presume you to be since Alexis is in Germany, you must make your own road. A man serves God in many ways. Your faith in Him is enough, as is my faith in you. Make your own way, choose your own life. Do not judge Ritoff, do not judge the Church, draw no conclusions that will embitter you. In your heart you will know what is right. You have always known. God will not fail you, nor will I'', his father's letter read.

Chapter Twenty-Three

THE taxi drove slowly through the evening traffic, stopping for lights, hedging through snarls of other cars, jolting its way toward the airport in the pale spring light.

This is the end of the trip, toward Claude. Just as those winter weeks of 1950 were the end of that other trip. Confused, hazy, unreal, those last weeks together, when everything happened at once, when everything that had been so easy, so natural, so like ourselves, turned upside down and left us disarmed and unready.

There was another taxi. We sat on either side of Nicole, rushing to hospital in the north of Paris. Jean had had a heart attack on the street. We sat white-faced and silent, not knowing how to comfort her, not knowing what to say, awkward in our silence.

Throughout a long night's vigil in the cold waiting-room of the hospital, while superior nurses bustled in and out without looking in our direction; waiting to be told that Jean would be all right, that it was not serious, because death was an unacceptable premise to us, waiting in the peeling ante-room, unheated and mildewed, till four o'clock in the morning. Finally a nurse appeared and said what we wanted her to say. He would live. He would live.

Then another taxi. Exhausted, relieved, shaky with the tears Nicole would not shed in front of us, and again the shabby hotel, fog-lit by the canal, and our own exhausted sleep afterward.

Days later Nicole began to close down the hotel. Jean was

going to live. But quietly, in the south. Or not at all. We nodded our heads, though we did not really understand.

Nicole, poor, mousy little Nicole, launched herself into papers, lawyers, *notaires*, *huissiers*, and all the incredible paraphernalia the French have invented to impede quick moves. Yet she managed, navigating craftily in a sea of red tape. Then, in a haze, between visits to Jean, grumbling weakly in his hospital bed, we looked about for a new home.

The shock of having to leave the hotel was lessened by our concern for Jean, but the shock was there none the less. For Mihailo the hotel was the only home he had known since he left his own in 1944. The white-walled room overlooking the canal, the bits of left-over furniture, the warmth we breathed into it, the gentle affection of Jean and Nicole, had given him a sense of love, of belonging that he had not known before in exile. Thus the move was all the more wrenching for him. Absently, he would touch the easel, the dresser, the window frame, during those last days; absently with a lingering gesture. I do not think he was even aware of doing it.

It had been such a private world. Few of our friends had ever been there. Claude, Serge, Teddy and Bob, that was all. The room, the hotel, our friendship with Jean and Nicole, were our own private province, quite apart from Montparnasse, or Saint-Germain-des-Prés. It was where we lived alone.

Of course, there was no question of finding another place up there in the north of Paris. Without Jean and Nicole the hotel ceased to exist. It and the canals would be left behind us. There was no alternative.

We were hopelessly innocent about looking for another place. Monique had rented her flat on the rue des Saints-Pères to a visiting university professor, so we no longer had that to fall back on. At first we tried to find an atelier but they proved to be outlandishly expensive. I looked at the ads in the *Herald Tribune* and the *Figaro*, but the prices were quite mad. We asked around, put up notices at the Dome and a few other cafés but nothing happened. Then, like so many others, we turned to the Left Bank hotels. If nothing else, they were close to the schools, close to the cafés, close to that other life we led.

With infinite sadness we began to move. We packed the pouf and the mirror, the blue-and-white striped curtains, the painting of the shepherdess in its huge plaster frame, a sizeable box of junky *bibelots* we had collected, and stored them in the Brooks' cellar. Monique and Fred were in Morocco. I hoped they would not mind.

Our last night in the room came. We ate dinner with Nicole, who was cheerful because of Jean's relatively speedy progress. She brought up a bottle of 1938 Veuve Cliquot from the cellar, to mark the occasion, and our spirits rose accordingly. Under the spell of the champagne Nicole gave us advice on how to deal with our new landlords, making us laugh like children with her comic descriptions of how hotel-keepers cheated innocents like ourselves.

We went upstairs to the naked room, indescribably bare without our Flea Market niceties. I did not want to look at it. We crawled into bed quickly, feeling an immense nostalgia already.

"From now on we will be like everyone else, living just anywhere," I said.

Mihailo laughed. "No, we won't. Anywhere we go will be home. Perhaps not so much as this, but home anyway. You will see. Think of how lucky we have been up to now! We will continue to have luck. God looks after us!"

Philippe came to get us in his car at ten the next morning. We piled up the back seat with suitcases, canvases, and clumsy cardboard boxes marked "Lait Gloria". Nicole dabbed her eyes now and then as she helped us down the stairs, repeating instructions about how to manage hotel life without her. Finally, when everything was packed away into the car, we looked at each other in farewell. She kissed us both, laughing and crying at the same time, and pushed us into the waiting car.

She stood at the door of the café. I turned back to wave and saw her there, pinched and grey in the yellow winter light, nodding her head as though she were learning a lesson and had finally understood its meaning.

Chapter Twenty-Four

THE hotel we moved into was in the rue Monsieur-le-Prince, near the corner of the rue Racine. We had a nice room, big and pleasant, but too dark to paint in. The landlady told us we could only have it until March 15th, it was reserved after that. Not painting made little difference, under those circumstances. We would have to continue to look around for a more permanent arrangement. For the time being, this was all we needed.

I realised with some surprise that we were short of money. We never had very much, but we were never really broke either. Tor had not sent anything since Christmas. However, the money I had made on the sale of the paintings kept us going. Mihailo had no money left from his savings—all he had was what he got for giving Russian lessons, not very much at best.

I had not heard from Tor since his holidays, except for one cable, though I had written him at length about the show. That was odd; I was the one who did not write, not Tor. One more link in the chain, the main link, about to be broken.

One after another, piece by piece. The next was Alexis.

I knew immediately who he was. Framed in the doorway, the dim light of the hotel hall cast uncertain shadows over him. Thin and stark, he appeared almost sinister in the semi-darkness. I smiled and extended my hand.

"You must be Alexis."

He took my hand in a cursory grasp and entered the room. "I was looking for Mihailo," he said, gazing around.

He spoke in English. With his great height, exaggerated by his slenderness and by the long, black overcoat he wore, he was a formidable presence. A mass of dark hair grew from a sharp widow's peak on his forehead. His nose was long and aquiline, his mouth thin, well shaped but held in a stern liplessness. His flat cheeks were clean-shaven but their very pallor suggested a beard. I thought of the Serb at Sarajevo for some reason. It was his eyes that made me think of the fanatic, his fiery, cold eyes, like bits of black dry ice on me, purposeful, permitting no contact other than on his own level. I was conscious of fear, perhaps for the first time in my life. For many many years after I have been awakened by dreams of those eyes piercing whatever complacency I've known, whatever security I've imagined to be mine. Implacable crusader, Alexis.

He sat down in the room's only armchair while I sat uncomfortably on the bed, aware that this was our bed and that Alexis would look at it and judge it as such. Judge it and judge me and his judgement would have no kindness, no indulgence.

I told him that Mihailo would be back in a few minutes, that he gave Russian lessons to two American girls on Thursdays and Saturdays. He nodded and took a cigarette from a pack I offered him. His hands were very white and long, rather beautiful.

"I went first to the seminary. The bishop told me of all this," he began. "Then Serge gave me the address of this hotel. Mihailo has not written in several months." His voice dropped.

I did not know what to answer. Not only was I intimidated by his presence but I was also afraid that he would misconstrue anything I might say. I nodded mutely.

"You are American, I am told." There was no edge to his voice yet the tone had altered imperceptibly. American, as though it were a disease.

"That's right. American." My voice with its back up. He smiled, a quick yet vague little smile, then looked at me for a moment. He put down the cigarette and began to talk.

"Mihailo has led what might be called a very protected life," he said slowly, his arms flat against his sides, his hands folded calmly on his crossed knees.

"Protected, despite the war and the camps and hospitals. Protected because others have sought to shield him. Even in the camps. There is an innocence in him that was unmistakable even to his captors, though they were not often given to character reading among their prisoners. Yet, they made an exception for Mihailo. And in the Seminary it was the same, though the poor bishop could not indulge his desire to protect his student as he would have liked to—you know, of course, that the seminary is operated on a below-subsistence level, largely on charity from parishes in America and Australia? Despite the bitter privations the bishop himself endures he tried to offer Mihailo a spiritual comfort far beyond his means." He cleared his throat, waiting perhaps for me to answer. I made no answer.

"The bishop failed. He blames himself for failing, which is understandable, I suppose. He is not a great man, I'm afraid, but neither is he a bad man. No. I do not think it is all that simple. Do you?"

His eyes had been wandering all over the room while he talked. He seemed to punctuate his remarks with looks like knife-thrusts into my eyes. Each look came unexpectedly, almost painfully. His final "do you?" found me unprepared. I felt myself showing an expression of hopeless disarray.

"Yet it is difficult to believe that it cannot all be worked out. Somehow," he continued. His eyes had sought mine but their intensity was unbearable and I lowered my gaze.

He went on; his voice seemed more relaxed, even detached, somehow reassuring:

"Exile is an unnatural predicament. It is totally distinct from emigration. There is only nostalgia in one but there is pain in the other. Mihailo became accustomed to pain too early in life to give it its just proportions, to accord it its deserved respect. Do I make myself clear? He has come to look at pain as an integral part of existence, but a part that it is now his duty, for the sake of survival, to outwit. He has learned through the years of living a marginal life to use subterfuge, to lean on expediency. He would not have done so in other circumstances but he has become forced to now in order to live. And in living, he has forgotten, or perhaps put aside, the proper perspective of his present and his future. Do I express myself clearly? It is difficult in English. I am so used to German now."

His tone had been pleasantly conversational, belying everything he had to say. There was no stridency, not at all. The harsh edge of his arrival seemed to have vanished. He smiled a little as he talked but I could see no warmth in his smile, no gentleness in his tone; it was as if what he meant as kind interest was merely an accomplished use of words. I was angry but did not dare show it for there was a violence in Alexis which frightened me.

"Your English is excellent," I said.

"Yet you hesitate to agree with me?" he smiled.

"I'm not sure I understand you."

"Yes, of course. That is only natural. It would be unnatural otherwise." He laughed in a curious way, not without humour and not really without warmth. I turned to look at him and he smiled reassuringly. Cat and mouse?

"What do you mean by expediency? What does expediency have to do with me?" I asked slowly, knowing that I was cornered and that the question was expected of me.

He rose and walked to the window. It had been raining. The slate roofs gleamed over the grey houses, ochres, blues, mauves played in the wet twilight. Someone was playing Arab music not far away.

Mihailo opened the door and found us standing there silently, each looking out of a window. His face was flushed with the cold and the fourth-floor climb had made him cough. There was a second of surprise, not altogether welcome surprise on his face, but it was instantly washed away and he gave an exuberant jump in Alexis's direction and there was much laughter and embracing. Alexis's face wore an expression of love and pleasure which startled me. I was too young for such subtleties, too inexperienced to deal with the complexities of emotion Alexis brought with him. I knew so instinctively and tried to brush them aside, make believe they were not there, continue as though he were just another Serb, not an enigmatic judge, not a wedge forcing himself between us. Had I been older, had we both been older, had even Alexis been older and less demanding, would it have been different?

They spoke Russian or Serbian or perhaps a mixture of both. Mihailo opened a bottle of wine to celebrate. The tension I had felt, had been made to feel before Mihailo arrived, had melted. Yet it was still Alexis who dominated the room. His face, his eyes bore an expression of concern, of love for Mihailo which excluded me and, though I had stopped being afraid of him, such concern worried me. That love would be a jealous love. Though I dismissed the notion of overt homosexuality I could not help wonder how healthy it was.

The conversation became general. They talked, now in English for my benefit, of our life in Paris, of the show, of Alexis's studies in Heidelberg and of his plans for the next few months. This latter news made me uncomfortable. Alexis was to remain in Paris till the summer, perhaps longer. A professor at the Sorbonne had become interested in him and would work with him on his thesis. Mihailo's enthusiasm was somewhat transparent to me. He was not prepared for Alexis, either. He has still not left the seminary, I thought. Not entirely. Mihailo was afraid of Alexis. I was sure of it. And comforted! As long as we were two to be afraid, as long as we were together in confronting Alexis, it would be all right. I relaxed in my chair and listened to them talk.

In those last few weeks, cold-ridden and uncertain, Alexis dominated our lives. Nothing seemed to be easy any more; worse than that, nothing seemed to be even possible. We spent so much time looking for a large enough hotel room for me to work in that there seemed to be no more free time for anything else. My letters to Tor remained unanswered. Our money was running low.

Alexis came to the hotel regularly. I formed a mental picture of him which will remain with me for the rest of my life. Gaunt, black—his coat, his hair, his frightening eyes, the shoulders of his coat often glistening with winter rain, he would appear at the hotel unannounced and assume control over us. Like two dutiful children, half mesmerised by this apparition, we would sit in uncomfortable hotel chairs and talk.

It took several such visits to get to the question of the seminary. Mihailo had mentioned having left it when Alexis first came but he merely nodded then and passed on to something else. Now he broached the subject himself. Mihailo seemed outwardly calm but the set of his mouth and chin belied such calm.

"I have seen the bishop, but you know that, I think," he began. "We talked about you a great deal. You know that had it been any of the others, Serge or Dimitri, it would have had little effect on the bishop. But you . . . he cannot reconcile himself to losing you. No. Not losing you. That is making it too simple."

He drew a figure in the air with his cigarette and his voice trailed off. Mihailo watched him, troubled.

"Not losing you. But failing you. That is more to the point. He failed you and you have been lost as a result of it. Moreover, he fears that you have lost your way, your way in life. Remember the bishop in Dubrovnik, Mihailo? How he wrote to your father about you, how he claimed that he had never had a pupil so obviously chosen for the religious life..."

"He was a sentimental old man. Besides, I was not even seventeen at the time and going through some kind of adolescent religious fever," Mihailo interrupted harshly, brushing the incident aside as though distasteful. He was frowning at Alexis.

"No. I was there. It was no adolescent fever," he replied softly. "Not then or ever." His tone was mild but he gave a ringing conclusiveness to his words.

I rose and went to a corner table and began to make sandwiches. They continued in Serbian. When the sandwiches were made I brought them over. Mihailo was pale, slumped in his armchair, wrung out. Alexis smiled at me almost gaily and began to arrange a place on the larger table for the sandwiches and the wine glasses.

His visits often ended on this note. Though even in his lightest moments he could never have been called entertaining, he did have a certain charm, a certain subdued gaiety which rose to the surface as Mihailo, slumped in a chair, receded into a quiet withdrawal. At first there was a kind of stubbornness in Mihailo's face but that, too, disappeared and he remained expressionless in the shadows till the conversation around the food and wine brought him back into the light. These little incidents never took very long—a quarter of an hour at most. But Mihailo seemed to be exhausted by them. Alexis never stayed long afterwards. When he had left, Mihailo often went to bed even though it was hardly ten o'clock, seeking in sleep a restorative as though from a terrible ordeal.

Claude came to Paris for a week. I suggested writing Alexis a note to tell him we would surely be out. Mihailo said it would not be necessary, he would tell him that afternoon.

"Do you see him in the afternoons?" I asked, surprised.

"He is at the Select every afternoon at five," he answered listlessly. "I sometimes see him when I go to meet you at the Grande Chaumière."

There was a split second when I had the feeling that Mihailo had found himself caught up in a trap and I had a panicked urge to run away, the two of us, anywhere—London, New York, away.

"He means well. You must try to understand . . ."

I had decided some time ago that Alexis was far too dangerous for me to allow him to come between us. As long as we were facing him together it would work out. I knew only too obscurely how much he affected Mihailo—how damaging is imperfect knowledge—and I was determined not to discuss him too much for fear that I would antagonise Mihailo.

I smiled a little and said, "He reminds me of an Ibsen play."

Claude's arrival brought us back to normal. The fact that Jean, Nicole and the Hotel du Midi were no longer there, the fact that we had moved into a chill, anonymous room and would soon have to move out of it into still another one, the fact that there was no hope of getting into the Sorbonne with a government grant this year—all that plus the unnerving presence of Alexis, had made us downcast, glum. Claude arrived and even the weather changed.

"Halcyon days!" he shouted from the train window. "Look at that sun!" Even our colds seemed to lift siege.

Claude stayed in our hotel. His mother's flat being rented he had no choice. I told him one morning when he walked with me to Montparnasse toward André Lhote's studio about Alexis. He did not take it as lightly as I thought he would nor did he say very much at the time. I suppose that he was as foreign as I to the world of religion and the bewildering pattern it took when it touched Mihailo. But he did meet Alexis. I wonder now whether it was as accidental as it seemed at the time.

We were at the Dôme one evening with a crowd of people. My back was to the door; Mihailo and Claude were facing it. I saw Mihailo stop short in the middle of a sentence and look up. There was something in his face,—fear, embarrassment, perhaps a little of both—which told me immediately that Alexis must be there. Claude's eyes were on someone behind me. His expression showed nothing but mild curiosity but his eyes were cold, appraising, interested. Mihailo made room for Alexis on the bench. There were introductions, someone ordered more drinks. In a noisy, crowded café among our friends, totally divorced from the atmosphere of the dingy hotel room and the disquieting light Alexis was able to cast upon it, he was a different figure.

Keep him out in the open, I thought, put him among my friends, and he takes on quite another form. I watched Mihailo to see whether he shared my reaction. He did not. Subdued, silent, he appeared to be listening to the conversation around him with only one ear.

Alexis turned to Claude and said: "I understand you are an actor."

Claude nodded, looking at his neighbour on the bench with undisguised curiosity. "And you?"

Alexis returned the look quite urbanely. He smiled. "I am doing a doctorate now. I would like to teach eventually."

"Teach what?"

"Ah yes. What indeed. Ethics, philosophy, morality, theology. What does it matter. Boring subjects for university students who would rather be somewhere else." He laughed and turned his long, dark head toward Claude who caught his eye and made a tiny, involuntary movement of recoil.

Mihailo rose suddenly, his face pale. "We should go now," he said, handing me my coat.

Claude rose, too, and Alexis, seated between them, was forced to get up to let Claude pass. We said goodbye to the others and the four of us walked to the door. I noticed that our places at the table had been taken before we left the café.

Outside it had begun to rain again. We said good night to Alexis and walked through the chill, wet streets to the hotel with only a half-hearted attempt at gaiety. That was the last time I saw Alexis. He never came to the hotel again. In any case, there was so little time left.

Chapter Twenty-Five

THE bright hall of Le Bourget with its clocks and polished surfaces, Formica counters and raucous loudspeakers seemed less real than when I had arrived early that morning. The expanses of gleaming floors dotted here and there with leather chairs and abstract-looking ashtrays seemed like an ad in the New Yorker. The cold click of my heels sounded hollow in my ears as I made my way to the bar.

My heart tightened as I saw Claude sitting at the bar. He lifted his head when he saw me, then rose. For the first time I noticed that Claude had aged. His face seemed tired, there were lines around his mouth. Tall, slender, his hair still abundant with just a touch of grey at the temples, he seldom looked his age, which was now thirty-nine. He kissed me lightly on the cheek.

There was nothing dramatic in the way our hands met or in the pressure of his body against mine. It was quite insanely matter-of-fact, as though we were at our local pub in Chelsea having a drink after the children were put to bed. But this was not the local and if my children were in bed it was not I who had put them there. Nor was Gavin with us as he usually was. No, there was nothing matter-of-fact in this meeting at a Paris airport, nothing that was not tinged with insanity and with failure.

He ordered drinks and we moved to a table by the window. Small lights flickered here and there on the runways, baggage trucks shuttled back and forth, people in uniforms darted across the tarmac, soundlessly, removed from my hearing by the thick plate glass. We were alone in the bar.

His face was expressionless, remote. There was no life in his remarkably beautiful grey eyes. He looked as unlike himself as I could ever have imagined. He looked ill.

"This is all highly dramatic," I began, not quite sure how to begin. He smiled.

"I know that and I'm sorry for the dramatics. But I was afraid you would somehow get to the truth alone. I . . . I didn't want you to do that. . . ."

He was looking away from me, his eyes on the lights outside on the runway.

"What could I have done? Look in the telephone book? Go to the church?" I smiled a little. "Actually, I was outside the church . . . Oh, for Christ's sake! What is it, Claude? Why didn't you want me to find out the truth alone? Why was it so important that you should be here? And how long have . . ."

"Wait. Let's begin by an easier question. Let's begin at the beginning." His voice was tired.

He continued. "As far as I'm concerned, the beginning was a letter from you around the end of April 1950. You had written me before, almost as soon as you arrived in Connecticut, and told me that Tor was dying. Your second letter in April was more . . . shrill. Not only was Tor dying but he was in hideous pain and you were alone with him and having to cope with all the decisions and details. But your main hysteria was not really that but was because Mihailo hadn't written once since you left Paris. You couldn't give in to panic because of the circumstances but your letter was so drenched in panic that I was alarmed.

"I wrote to Philippe and to your friend Aggie and asked them to find out what had happened. I wrote to Mihailo myself, at the seminary, care of Serge, but I got no answer. Philippe and Aggie both wrote back within a fortnight saying that they had found no traces of Mihailo anywhere. Aggie remembered seeing him chatting with a group of Yugoslavs at the Select. She went to the Select and asked around and someone told her he had a cousin who would know but the cousin had gone to Heidelberg. Perhaps Mihailo had gone with him? That seemed logical enough to me and to Aggie as well. She said that she would continue to enquire at the Select and should anything turn up, she would write you directly.

"I could easily see Mihailo going to Germany with Alexis but I could not understand why he had not written you. Nevertheless, I thought it would be a good idea to minimise any importance this might have and wrote you something vague. You did not answer for another four weeks or so. By that time Tor was near death and you seemed in a state of shock. Mihailo had not answered any of your letters, you were half out of your mind and your letter to me was almost incoherent. I took the next boat train to Paris.

"The first mistake I made was to go to that church. They told me a lie that was the key to it all. They told me that Serge had left the seminary. Had I gone there asking for Serge directly instead of asking for Mihailo, all this would... Well, be that as it may. That is the way it did happen. I got nowhere at the Seminary. They were rude, unhelpful and all but threw me out.

"Then, of course, I saw Alexis. I told you about Alexis, about meeting him at the Select and about his flat comment as I was ready to leave—'Didn't it ever occur to Carola that Mihailo might have had enough?' Well, frankly, it did occur to me. Not before. But after he said it. I left him and began to walk. The more I thought of it the more logical it seemed. Look at it this way and you'll see what I mean. You left Paris when Mihailo was under stress. Alexis's presence was a constant reminder of what he had planned as his life since boyhood. Even if Alexis had exerted no pressure on him whatsoever—and I know that was not the case—but even had it been so, Alexis's mere presence could have, would have been enough to awaken all his doubts, to fire all his misgivings. I could see how it might have been after you left.

"Alexis managed to wield an increasingly unbearable pressure on him to try and go back to the seminary, not necessarily this one but any one. Why not Germany, after all? Perhaps they are better subsidised there. Anyway, I could see it quite clearly. His line of argument would go something like this. Why not try, why not try to reconcile himself with his God, without . . . interferences. Why not test his decision to leave the seminary which was taken, as we all know, in anger and mainly because of the bishop's intractable character. There is nothing, after all, to prevent him now that he is free . . . No, don't interrupt me. I know it sounds unlikely but since his silence was even more unlikely, the hypothesis was not all that far-fetched.

"The more I thought of it and the more I thought of Alexis, in terms of his own character and in terms of the influence he held over Mihailo, it did make a certain amount of sense.

"Look at it this way. When you met Mihailo and drew him into your life you did two things: you gave him love and affection and the key to a new world, a world which not only was unknown to him before but which was of no interest to him before. Secondly, you placed him before a choice . . . retaining his old values, or rather retaining the pattern of his life as he had set it before meeting you, or else accepting you and whatever future you could make together *on your terms*. No, don't protest. I know you had never put it in that light but whether you were conscious of it or not that is how an outsider would see it. Surely—and think carefully now— surely that is how Alexis saw it?

"If you recall, Alexis never openly opposed you. His hostility was clothed in a sort of alarming friendship for you. What he said to Mihailo when you were not there we will never know and what he said to Mihailo after you went to the States we will know even less. But Alexis was the catalyst. It was he who moved the figures and when he said to me, 'Mihailo has had enough', I somehow realised that, though it was crudely phrased, that might well be the answer.

"There was no way of reaching Mihailo. Alexis had seen to that. I could hardly go to the police. I did, of course, check all the people and places I could think of and I drew blanks all round. I had to accept Alexis's word! By then I was more than ready to punch him in the nose. There was something so bloody oriental about the whole thing! I felt helpless, unable to cope with whatever Byzantine dialectic Alexis had used and, somehow, I was suddenly afraid of him. I went back to the Select on the night I was to leave for London. One of the waiters told me he had left for Heidelberg that morning. So I never got to see him again.

"Well, I wrote you as gently as I could that Mihailo seemed to have disappeared, that he left no traces anywhere and, believe me, Carola, I wrote ten drafts of that letter before sending it . . . I suggested that you try to adjust to the situation as it was.

"I know what followed. Your mother wrote me and we corresponded regularly over the next few years. I knew about your running away, I knew about your jobs, about the analyst and I knew when you seemed to emerge into some kind of healthier reality. I wanted to go to you several times but your mother dissuaded me. She, her husband, the analyst, all of them seemed convinced that I would do more harm than good. I don't know why and I don't know to this day whether I was right in listening to them. But while I was still wavering, you seemed to get better and were working and the urgency seemed to have gone out of it. Then Gavin was going over and I suggested he see you and, you will pardon me for laughing, he did what I had very much in the back of my mind to do all along . . . marry you. Oh, come now. Don't look so surprised."

But I did look surprised. His face clouded and the pain that was there before was more poignant.

"I might as well be honest. It can't matter to any of us now. Before Mihailo came into it we were still very much in the last throes of adolescence and I for one had no interest whatsoever in marriage. Then came Mihailo and, well, that was that. But when you left, when all this mess was at its thickest, I realised that I was far more attached to you than I had ever wanted to admit. I also realised that my indecision in going to New York was based more on my fears of finding you still so . . . so involved with Mihailo that I would be forced to resume my old role of bosom pal. Which, I'm afraid, I would have found painful to maintain. It wasn't really what your mother and the head-shrinker said, it was what my own heart said . . ."

He paused and took a deep drink, then lit a cigarette, avoiding my eyes. I was surprised but, after all, not really that surprised. I didn't say anything. There was too much to say now.

"Anyway," he continued with a wry grin, "old dark-horse Davies, to whom I had told just the barest details about you and Mihailo, arrived on the scene and packed you up in his slide-rule case and that was that. At first I was furious, sick with rage at my own hesitations. But then I saw that, at least from your point of view, it was all for the best. Gavin was an outsider, had no connection with Paris, was a healthy no-nonsense Welshman with a heart that big and an apparently inexhaustible supply of sons . . . Which, in a way, was what you needed. He was clever enough to realise it and I was sport enough to accept it. And that was that.

"But when you came back to London, the night you arrived . . . I was thrown right back to the very beginning.

You still loved Mihailo. Despite the five years, despite Gavin, despite the babies, you still loved him! And then suddenly and sickeningly the whole tissue of explanations I had accepted up to then fell away at my feet. I saw you and saw in your eyes the same light I had seen in Mihailo's and I was utterly convinced that what I had believed up to then to be a reasonable explanation for an unreasonable situation was a pack of filthy lies. I flew to Paris three days later and in just a few hours I found out the truth."

There were fewer lights on the runways but they were brighter than before. Claude's voice had dropped. He drained his glass and beckoned for another. I was astonishingly calm. My heart was still and I felt curiously rested. It was almost as though I knew what he was going to say next. The emotions that crossed Claude's face, the torn expression in his eyes, in his mouth, moved me but I felt somehow detached from him. I was not numb, not exactly, nor was I quite with him either. It had been a long day. It had been a long fifteen years. Perhaps it was too late. Perhaps I had been numb too long.

"How do you feel?" he asked. "Do you want me to go on or would you rather we drove into town?" He looked out across the airport lounge, then turned his eyes quickly back to me, unsure.

"Please go on," I said, "I'm all right. I'm really all right."

"In 1955 I flew over and I took a taxi straight to the church ready to fight my way through it if necessary. But it proved quite unnecessary. There was a new man there, a younger man who spoke very good French. The place was quite changed; it looked well kept, prosperous. This was, after all, five years later.

"I was shown into a pleasant library. The priest and I sat down. I told him that I was trying to trace a former student, Mihailo Kerovitch, or, if that proved too difficult, a friend of his whose name was Serge. He looked startled. I began to apologise but he cut me short.

"'You mean Serge Voitich, I suppose. Yes, I can help you. I can give you his address. He lives not far from here, as a matter of fact.' The man's voice was slow and his face troubled. There was a silence between us, a heavy silence. Carola, in that silence I suddenly knew what had happened."

Claude's eyes seemed to burn through me but I was beyond his reach. The wild thumping of my heart filled the air around me. I made no move. My hands were frozen on the table. I was no help to Claude. He looked out at the flickering lights, his face pale. I would have liked to say something, anything, to him but there were no words near me.

"The priest stood up and began pacing around the room. Finally, he said, 'All this was before my time. I know Serge because he is a member of my congregation . . . it was five years ago. I was not here then.' He turned toward me. 'Why did you come? What have you to do with this?' I didn't answer. He stared at me hard then in a quiet, almost gentle voice he said, 'Mihailo Kerovitch committed suicide. He hanged himself in a sanatorium in the Alps in November of 1950.'"

Claude's words fell flat around my hands on the table. Nothing moved, neither he nor I nor the still air we breathed. Motionless, the words remained at my fingertips waiting to be retrieved, to be put into place, to be translated into meaning, to take on form and colour, to grow into tangible shape in the cup of my two still hands.

I sat there alone for some time contemplating the words. Slowly and imperfectly they seemed to rise and drift away, pockets of smoke, leaving me behind.

Claude's eyes were full, his hands shaking as he reached for mine. What he said now seemed unimportant.

Chapter Twenty-Six

WE walked from the bar through the airport doors and the wind struck our faces with unexpected vigour. In the taxi we sat close together, our hands entwined, but silent. Claude's hands were cold, his face ashen. I suddenly realised how much strength he had needed all these years to keep this from me. But why? Why had he done so?

"Why have you never told me?" I asked.

"I was going to then, in 1955. But when I came back from Paris you were in Wales and when you finally came back from Wales, Gavin told me you were pregnant again. So I decided to wait. Then, the longer I waited the harder it became. So ultimately, seeing you so often, seeing you with the children, with Gavin, absorbed in the present, so painfully absorbed in the present, I simply didn't have the heart—or is it the guts?—to open the whole thing all over again."

I tried to ask him to continue but somehow the words would not come.

Sensing this, he said, "Shall I go on?"

I nodded my head.

"The priest could see what a shock it had been. He brought over a bottle of brandy and two glasses. We drank in silence. There was little else he knew but he suggested calling Serge. It was early evening and Serge happened to be at home. He joined us in less than twenty minutes. Serge knew the whole story.

"When you left Paris Mihailo had a cold. But it was not just a cold and he suspected as much. He had seen enough TB cases to recognise the symptoms in himself. Had that week of uncertainty about Tor's illness not taken place, he would have gone for a medical check-up. But when it became clear that you would have to leave he put it off. He packed your things, brought them round to Mother's storage bins and told Serge, who had helped him do the moving, that he was going to stay with Alexis. Serge went with him to the rue Huysmans where Alexis had a room on the sixth floor, saw him settled and then left. Alexis took over.

"We can only guess what happened next. Alexis took advantage of Mihailo's physical exhaustion to persuade him that this separation from you was a God-given opportunity to break the ties for good, to put his infatuation with you to the test. For in his heart Alexis was honestly and completely convinced that it was no more than that—an infatuation with a light-headed American girl who had no place whatsoever in Mihailo's life which was and always had been dedicated to God.

"That Alexis was a frustrated mystic is only too clear and that he projected his own impossible ambitions into Mihailo is even clearer. But in all fairness to him, he was certainly never aware of what the final consequences could have been; what indeed they were.

"Mihailo was feverish, exalted and depressed in turns. Cooped up in that little room with Alexis's constant pressure made him even worse. He wrote you several letters giving them to Alexis to post. Alexis never did, of course. When Serge brought around your letters it was Alexis who took them. He never let Serge in the room—either he said that Mihailo was sleeping or had gone out or gave some other excuse, but always a plausible one. Serge never guessed that he was being kept away deliberately. Nor did he guess that Alexis was, in effect, sequestering Mihailo in order to purge him of his infatuation. But Mihailo's health intervened.

"Several weeks later Serge went around again with more

letters and Alexis told him Mihailo was away, had got a job on a farm for the summer—this was May. That, too, was plausible. Alexis took the letters promising to forward them. When Serge asked for Mihailo's address, Alexis told him that there was no fixed address, that he went from farm to farm. Serge again swallowed it.

"But why should he have questioned it? He knew that Mihailo adored this rather forbidding cousin and, though Serge didn't share his enthusiasm, he respected Mihailo's affection. They were cousins, were they not? And in exile cousins were more attached to each other than they might have been at home. Those boys lived disinherited lives; any link with their roots, with their homes, was to be respected far beyond any friendship made in exile.

"But the truth was somewhat different. Mihailo's illness was too serious by the end of April to procrastinate any longer. Alexis got him admitted to the student's hospital at the Cité Universitaire and from there he was sent to a sanatorium in the Alps near Grenoble. Alexis was alarmed, of course, but the doctors were reassuring. He was very ill for several months but essentially Mihailo was a healthy boy and in time he began to improve. Yet, the doctors were not satisfied. They felt he was holding back, refusing to be reached. He responded to treatment only to a certain extent, no further. They wrote to Alexis as his nearest relative but they minimised the situation, for Mihailo had made it clear to the doctors that he would refuse to see Alexis even if he should make the trip. He became increasingly withdrawn, uncooperative, silent. He refused absolutely to talk to the resident psychiatrist. He simply did not want to get better.

"Alexis went to see him late in the summer and Mihailo had no choice but to see him. They spoke, reluctantly at first, but finally very frankly. Mihailo told Alexis that he no longer thought of you, that you had used your father's illness as a pretext for getting rid of him, that once in America you saw what an impossible marriage theirs would have been. He told Alexis that he had been a fool to have taken you seriously but since he had always taken everything seriously, coming from a long line of serious asses, it was not all that much of a surprise. Alexis was somewhat shaken by his bitterness but put it down to the usual heartache after a first love affair. A common enough disease and seldom fatal. But he was more seriously shaken when Mihailo's bitterness extended to the Church, to God. His faith had been destroyed and he would not even speak in terms of the Church or of belief or of faith in any form. He said he was delighted to see the Communists stamp out whatever remained of religion in Eastern Europe and told Alexis that he hoped they would cross the Adriatic and start on Rome.

"He scandalised Alexis. Unfortunately, Alexis could not see the trees for the forest, however. His anti-Communist soul was so disturbed by Mihailo's ranting that he did not stop to think that the boy was totally off-balance and somewhat out of his mind.

"Alexis was also suffering from something he could not quite understand in himself: guilt. And that, if you like, explains everything. For a time he thought of going back to the Sana and explaining to Mihailo what he had done with the letters—not mailing his and destroying yours—but he was too confused by Mihailo's multiple hostilities and, frankly, he was afraid of what Mihailo's reaction might be. The weeks passed and Alexis in his hopeless, guilt-ridden quandary, waited for things to get better. Mihailo seldom wrote. Alexis had very little money then but he telephoned to the Sana as often as he could just to reassure himself. The doctor's reports were erratic, like the boy's recovery itself. He had ups and downs which confused them, even though TB is a classically confusing disease.

"Then towards autumn, he calmed down. He wrote to Alexis apologising for having been such a bother, for having been unreasonable and such a source of anxiety. Alexis breathed easily for the first time since you left.

"He was not insensitive to the dangers of his position. He knew the risks he had taken in playing God. Yet he had this burning faith in Mihailo's vocation and he had the fanatic's iron-clad conviction that he was right. Though he had wavered many times during the summer, seeing Mihailo's sufferings and fearing that his mental state would affect his physical recovery, he took heart at the news that the nightmare seemed to be ended. He had been right to do what he had done! He had been right to force Mihailo out of your world and back into his own; the dangers had been many, the pain intense but he was right and he had prevailed.

"Mihailo became very easy to handle in the Sana, good-humoured and considerate. His lungs were healing, he was allowed to take walks in the good weather. All the progress that he had refused to make over the previous six months he seemed to make in a few short weeks. The doctors were delighted.

"Indeed, they were all immensely shocked when he was found hanging from a tree one sunny November morning with a rosary coiled around his wrist."

Claude's voice dropped. His hands were still, his eyes turned away from me.

All this time, all this time of mourning. All these years of searching. He had been dead all these years.

There were no tears now. No tears in a foreign taxi, in an alien land. No tears now for a wasted life and a broken one, for two stunted lives cut short by different meanings of love, by insufficient meanings of love. Alexis loved Mihailo, too. Could he be blamed? Was his life not broken, too? Did he thrive and prosper on Mihailo's grave? Of course not. Who can blame Alexis more than he blames himself? Who can blame me for having been too young and too eager, ignorant of men's love of God, ignorant of everything but our own love for each other, ignorant of the terrible dangers of love?

We left the taxi at my hotel and sat down in the deserted lounge. It was an oddly impersonal place to finish talking, the empty lounge of a hotel, but somehow it was fitting. As though Mihailo had been removed from the recesses where I had held him all these years, secret unto myself, my own fulfilment hidden from everyone else, my own hurt, my own love. Empty now, I listened to Claude.

"Alexis took the news alone. He was the only one to know. He suffered terribly because it was his own work, it was he who murdered Mihailo. Then he did a remarkable thing. He brought the body back to Yugoslavia himself. Which, of course, was another kind of suicide. He was a refugee and the Tito government was hardly amenable to refugees at that time. Before leaving he wrote a long explanation of what had happened to Serge. Then he went back to Belgrade and, as he expected, was arrested shortly after. He spent several years in prison but was released eventually and he now teaches elementary school somewhere in the provinces.

"That was his expiation. Mihailo is buried in his father's churchyard and his family knows nothing of the circumstances of his death. They think it was tuberculosis.

"Serge, when he received Alexis's letter, was too stunned to think straight. He did not know how to reach you or whether to reach you. After weeks of indecision, when he too had left the seminary, he came to the conclusion that it would be better that you didn't know. Your letters to Mihailo had long since ceased to come. He felt that you had accepted the break and felt that this added burden would be unnecessary. So, for a very long time, he told no one. When the new priest came to the church several years later, Alexis's name came up in conversation. Alexis's return to Yugoslavia, to jail, was a subject of speculation. Serge, on the spur of the moment, told the priest the whole story. I came along just a few months later. That was in 1955."

He seemed exhausted. It was very late, his eyes were red, his face haggard. There was nothing more to say.

Tomorrow morning we will return to the airport together. Then Claude will take me in another taxi to the plane and we will fly home to London to my children, my husband, my home and all these years which have been washed away tonight. All these thirteen years of my left-over life will fall back into place and there will be no room for mourning, no room for tears.

All the years will fit back into shape as if this day had never been and no one will know how second-best, how insufficiently second-best they are. And always have been! No one but myself. No mourning but my own for a death gone too long unmourned, a death which was my own.

Later in my room I will cry, alone in my room. Later when Claude has gone, his tired face, his uncertain words no longer with me, demanding of me an answer, a word, a nod, when he has gone then I will cry. Feeling the hand of that boy who walked with me by the canals in the yellow light of winter, feeling in my hand his long fingers and strong young hand in mine, then I'll cry. Long and loud, released from all the years in between, I'll cry.